Milkman

DAN HOLOHAN

© 2018 Dan Holohan

All rights reserved. No part of this publication may be reproduced or used in any form or by any means – graphic, electronic or mechanical, including photocopying, recording, taping, or information storage and retrieval systems, or posting on the Internet – without written permission of the publisher. So there.

*For all the young ones
who see more than they can bear*

Delaney's
2018

"You look like a cat guy," she said. "Am I right?"

He had just sat on the stool. Her question made him laugh.

"That a bartender question?" he said.

"Yep," she said. "It's good to know whether a guy is a cat guy or a dog guy on a slow afternoon. So which is it?"

"Cat," he said.

"See how good I am?" she said. "What can I get you?"

He looked at the taps. "Stella," he said.

"Cats and Stella. You have a well-balanced soul," she said, reaching for a pint glass.

"You're good," he said.

"Thank you, young man," she said, letting loose a throaty laugh.

He smiled. "What's your name?"

"Apple."

"Seriously?"

"Yep," she said.

"Is that a nickname?"

"It is."

"For what?"

"Apollonia."

"I like it," he said.

"Apollonia or Apple?" she said.

"Both of them."

"Thanks."

"What does Apollonia mean?" he said.

"I'm not sure you're ready for that," she said.

"I can take it."

"It means destruction," she said and winked.

"Let's go back to Apple," he said.

"Good choice," she said.

"What sort of apple are you?"

"Delicious," she said and smiled.

"I suppose I'm not the first person to ask that question," he said and smiled.

"Nope, and if you were an old lady I would have said Granny Smith," she laughed.

"You have a nice laugh, Apple."

"Thanks."

"And a nice smile."

"Thanks again."

"How long has this place been called Delaney's?"

"About six months."

"Who owns it?"

"Keith Jennings. He's a good guy. He spent a ton of money fixing it up. Check out the bathrooms. You'd think you were in a fancy restaurant instead of a neighborhood bar."

"Did Mr. Jennings name it Delaney's?"

"Yep."

"So who's Delaney?"

"Who knows? But who doesn't love an Irish bar? Maybe Delaney will show up here and buy us both a drink."

He laughed. "What was it before it was Delaney's? I've been away for a while."

"It was called Suds and Darts. Cheap beer and a couple of dart boards, which I heard they got rid of not long after the place opened because there were too many fights over the dart games."

"But they kept the same name?"

"Yeah. Maybe they were too cheap to change the sign." She shrugged.

"I guess they had a young crowd?" he said.

"Too young. There were fights in here every night. They wrecked the place. Punched holes in the bathroom walls, busted the sink and the toilet a bunch of times. A plumber friend told me that. They threw up and urinated on the side of the building, and even out front. Right out there in the street." She pointed out the wide window. "The cops were in here all the time. The owner kept getting fined for serving the underaged kids from the college."

"That's no way to run a business," he said.

"No, it's not," Apple said. "They finally shut him down and he just walked away from it. It was empty for about a year before Keith bought it from the bank and fixed it up. We're getting a nice crowd now. We don't allow kids in here."

"I used to come in here back in the Sixties," he said.

"Really?" Apple said. "We were talking about that the other day, me and a couple of the locals. I like working the afternoons. Good people come in for a drink. Older people."

He smiled.

"But none of them were living around here that far back, so no one knew about this place in the Sixties. I mean what it was then. I know it's been a neighborhood bar for a long time but no one remembered its name from back then."

"It was called The Landing Strip."

"Really? As in airplanes?"

"Yes. Grumman was in Bethpage. Republic was in Farmingdale. Well, at least it was until Fairchild Hiller bought the company in Sixty-seven. This place was right between those two big airplane manufacturers. They both built war planes so there was plenty of business because there was plenty of war, both hot and cold. The workers would come in here after their shifts, which went around the clock. Their landing strip was right here." He tapped the empty stool next to him and smiled.

"I like that name," she said. "The Landing Strip. It sounds homey."

"It was a good place. It opened early and closed late. Tap beer was twenty cents for a shortie."

"What's a shortie?" Apple said. "That a Sixties thing?"

"You've never seen a shortie? It's a small, thin beer glass. It holds just eight ounces. Fits in the palm of your hand, like a handlebar grip. It was just the right size for a beer."

"That's not much beer for a serious drinker," Apple said. "It's all pints nowadays."

"I know, but a serious drinker would have a lot of them, and with the shortie, your beer never got warm. The bartender kept filling them up, again and again. Nothing but cold beer. It was nice."

"Sounds like a lot of work for the bartender. Gimme the pints," Apple laughed.

"Well, maybe it was a lot of work, but back then, it was all about the chat. No TVs in the bar. A bartender wouldn't even ask if you wanted another. If your glass was empty, he just filled it, chatting all the time. He'd be picking up the dollar bills, putting down the quarters, nickels, and dimes as change. Nobody ran a tab, or paid with a credit card in those days. It was all cash on the bar and it went on all day long and on into the night. Lots of good talk. It didn't stop until you got up off your stool and went home."

"I think talking makes people drink more," Apple said as he took a sip.

He choked back a laugh.

"Thanks a lot!" he said, wiping his mouth with the back of his hand.

"Sorry," she said, laughing.

"You would have done well in here back in the day."

"You think so?"

"I do."

"Did they serve mixed drinks back then?" Apple said. "I mix a mean drink."

"Not really," he said. "It was mostly just draft beer and shots. Rye whiskey cost a half-buck. But back then, people weren't making much money, so I guess a half-buck is relative. Most guys would have a shot with every fourth or fifth beer, and every fourth beer was a buy-back. On the house. The bartender kept all of that in his head."

"That's not an easy thing to do," Apple said. "And they sold whiskey in here for just fifty cents? Gosh."

"*Rye* whiskey," he said.

"We don't even have rye whiskey," Apple said, glancing back at the bottles.

"It was Fleischmann's Straight Rye back then," he said. "Cheap stuff, but it went well with the beer. And with a smoke, of course. No one worried about cancer then. I never smoked, but I may be the only one my age who can say that."

"I never worked a bar where people smoked," Apple said.

"Well, that was then. The air got pretty nasty in here," he said, looking at the ceiling. "It used to be nicotine-yellow up there."

"And you were a part of all of that?" Apple said. "You don't look that old."

"Oh, I'm old. I had my first beer in this place on my eighteenth birthday. That was the drinking age back then. Eighteen. I never had a drink before that day."

"You were a good boy," Apple said. Real nice smile.

"I was. And I did as I was told."

"Always?"

"Well, most of the time," he laughed.

"And you drank with the old guys who built the airplanes."

"Yes, the war planes. And, yes, those guys were all older than I was, that's for sure. They'd probably seem young to me now. They had great stories. And the bar wasn't long like this one is now. It was a semicircle back then. It went from over there to over there." He pointed.

"That must have been nice," Apple said.

"It was. Everyone could see everyone else; and the bartender didn't have far to walk between drinkers."

"I like that," Apple said.

"And you could overhear everyone else's chat because of the big semicircle, and if you had something to add, you just joined in. We all got along, mostly. I mean there were a few guys who liked to bust chops, but you get that in every bar."

"Tell me about it," Apple said.

"And there was a house cat named Fiona. She sat on the windowsill when it was sunny. She was very social and she liked to walk across the bar. The guys would pet her as she went by. Tug her tail a bit. She liked that. She wasn't afraid of anyone and

I guess she caught an occasional mouse to earn her keep. I don't think you could get away with having a bar cat nowadays."

"The Board of Health would probably shut us down," Apple said.

"It was a different time."

"So how old are you?" Apple said.

"I'm seventy."

"No way!"

"Well, I was the last time I checked," he laughed. "God's truth."

"You sure fooled me. Your hair's not even gray. I figured you were maybe fifty. Fifty at the *most*."

"I used to be fifty, but that was a long time ago."

"Do you dye your hair?"

"Me? No. I don't know why it stays brown." He rubbed his hair. It had a smooth feel to it as he moved his palm back and forth on it. "Genetics, I guess. It does have its drawbacks, though. I don't always get the senior discounts. I have to show my ID, just like I had to show my draft card when I was eighteen. Life's one big circle, I guess." He smiled. "How old are you, Apple?" he said.

"I'm forty."

"I remember forty. That was a looong time ago."

"Was it good for you?" Apple said, winking.

"It was better than eighteen, that's for sure. I was pretty confused at eighteen. The Sixties were a confusing time."

"Sounds like there's a story there," Apple said.

"There's a story everywhere," he said.

"Tell me a good one." Apple leaned over the bar and rested on her forearms. Smiled.

11

"Okay. There was a bartender who had your job once upon a time. His name was Richie. Richie was bone-skinny and he slicked back his hair with Brylcreem, like the guys in the Fifties did. Do you know what Brylcreem is?"

"Sure."

"If you do, then I think you would have liked Richie's car."

"What did he drive?" Apple said.

"He had a Sixty-six Mustang coupe. Silver-blue-metallic and showroom fresh. I was so jealous of that car."

"Wow," Apple said. "I wonder if that car is still around."

"I like to think so," he said. "It would be worth a lot today. But who knows?"

"It would be fun to go looking for it," Apple said.

"Is that an invitation to a road trip?" he said, smiling. "You'd better be darn sure if it is, and know what you're getting into."

That throaty laugh again. It made him want to stay there forever.

"So what happened?" Apple said when she caught her breath. "Story please."

"Well, Richie was here nearly all the time. He worked from three in the afternoon until four in the morning. I don't know how he did it. He'd lock the place up when the last drinker went home and then he'd sleep it off on the backseat of the Mustang, right out there at the curb." He pointed. Apple turned to look. "That was back in the day when the bartenders used to drink with their customers."

"We can't get away with that now," Apple said.

"No, and I suppose that's a good thing. But back then, it was anything goes."

"Hard to believe," Apple said.

"Right?"

"For sure."

"I'd see him every morning when I was going by at about six o'clock. I'd tap on the Mustang's window to wake him up so he could get home. He always said that two hours sleep was all he needed to sober up and drive home. I don't know where he lived, but he said it wasn't far from here, and even if the cops stopped him, they probably would have let him go with a warning. That's just the way it was back then. They knew Richie from the bar. I'd give him a quart of orange juice to get him started on his way every morning. He'd have to be back to work before you knew it, and I never saw the guy eat food. Not even once. He was so skinny."

"Maybe he had an eating disorder," Apple said.

"Maybe. Or maybe he had ulcers. We never talked about it. It was just something I noticed."

"Where'd you get orange juice at that hour?" Apple said. "And what were you doing there so early?"

"I was a milkman in those days. I'd go right by the bar when I was near the end of my route. I always had orange juice on the truck. We delivered the milk and the juice. Oh, and the eggs, the butter, the cream, and all the other good stuff too. We brought it all right to your door."

"That's nice, but what made you do that? Stop by here to give him orange juice, I mean," Apple said.

He shrugged. "I don't know. I guess I just liked the guy. He was always good to me. He treated me like a man in here, even though I was still a boy in so many ways. When I needed advice, he was always good for it. He never made fun of me, even if I asked stupid questions. I liked bringing him juice, and he was grateful for it."

13

"That's nice," Apple said. "I didn't know there used to be milkmen around here. I always thought that was an out-in-the-country thing."

"No, we were definitely here," he said. "There were a bunch of us."

"Did you wear a white uniform with one of those cute caps?" She smiled.

"Nah," he laughed. "We never dressed like that. We wore clothing appropriate for the weather. Layers in the winter. Shorts in the summer. Oh, and good shoes year round. A milkman lived on his feet. It was move, move, move. Get the milk in the milk boxes before the ice melted. Every day was a race to finish fast."

"Did you see many people in the middle of the night?"

"Hardly anyone," he said.

"Were you lonely?"

"Never. I listened to the radio a lot."

"Rock and roll?"

"No, early talk radio. Long John Nebel."

"So today I'm hanging with a genuine milkman from back in the day who listened to early talk radio. Whoda thunk it?"

"I know, right?"

"So what happened to all you guys?" Apple said.

"The supermarkets put us out of business. And that happened real fast. We never saw it coming. One day, we were a part of everyone's life; and then the next day we were the dairy equivalent of vinyl records. We just disappeared." He tipped back his beer.

"Ready?" Apple pointed at his glass.

"Sure," he said. "I wish you could drink with me. I hate drinking alone."

Apple looked around. It was just the two of them.

"Oh, what the hell," she said. "Let's keep it our secret."

"Mum's the word," he said and smiled.

Apple reached for a fresh pint glass, but he slid his old one toward her.

"Use this one," he said. "It's less work for you."

"That's nice. Thanks. You're a good guy."

Apple poured herself a Pinot Grigio in a ceramic coffee mug and drew another draft for him.

"So tell me about your cat," she said.

"Ahh, Fiona," he said. "She's been gone for many years, but she was the queen of cats in her day."

"Wait a minute, are you talking about the bar cat?"

"Yes."

"She was yours?"

"Not at first, but she adopted me."

"Nice," Apple said. "Cats don't adopt just anyone. You must be very special."

"Well, Fiona thought so."

"Was she your only cat?"

He nodded. "My one and only. Nothing could replace Fiona."

"And after all these years, you still call yourself a cat guy?"

"Hey, *you* called me a cat guy," he laughed. "I just pled guilty."

An older man hobbled in. He worked his way onto a stool at the far end of the bar and laid his cane across the two empty stools beside him. Apple walked down to him, stopping along the way to pull a longneck Bud out of the cooler, no glass. The man didn't have to ask for it, He nodded, and then he turned his

15

attention to FOX News on the TV. The sound was off but the subtitles were on.

    She walked back down the bar. He counted her steps. Seven. She had a model's stride.

    "So what happened to Richie?" she said.

    "We done talking cats?" he smiled.

    "For now. Tell me about what happened to Richie. He's where the story started."

    "I wish I knew what happened to him," he said. "I stopped by with his orange juice one morning and his car was gone. I went to the bar later that afternoon and the owner was bartending. I never saw Richie again. That's the day Fiona adopted me," he said.

    "She just go home with you?"

    "Yes," he said.

    "Story please?" she said.

    He smiled. "One story at a time."

    "Okay." Apple smiled. "So you're telling me you never went back to the bar again. Why not?"

    "I don't know. It just felt like that part of my life was over. And I never saw the Mustang again. I drove by every morning near the end of my route and I never saw it again." He glanced out the window. "That was such a sweet car."

    "What do you think happened to Richie?" Apple said.

    "Life," he said.

    She sipped her wine. Nodded.

    The old man at the end of the bar coughed hard. Wheezed. Apple looked over at him. "You okay?" He waved her off.

    She waited a full minute. Watched him cough.

He waved her off again, without looking away from FOX News.

"So what brings you back now?" she said.

"Beats me," he said. "I haven't been in this place for fifty-two years. I've been away. I just moved back recently and I was passing by. I figured it was time to stop in for a cold one."

"Are you glad you did?" Apple said. "I'm glad you did."

"We'll see," he said and smiled.

He took a long sip of his beer, turned on his stool, and stared out the window to where the silver-blue-metallic Mustang used to gleam in the dawn. Richie stretched across the backseat, fast asleep.

He stared. Said nothing.

Apple laced her fingers around her mug, like she was holding a January hot chocolate. She shifted her weight to her other foot. Waited.

Bit her lower lip.

Glanced at the old man at the end of the bar again, still glued to the TV.

She lifted the mug with both hands and sipped.

Waited.

Waited for him to come back to her.

Waited.

She glanced down the bar again.

The man was staring at her.

She looked away.

Wednesday Morning 3 A.M.

Brian McKenna never really thought about the water and where it came from. It just flowed from the faucets and went down the drain. Turn the knobs and there it was. Cold on the right, hot on the left. No need to think about it. It was just there, like breathing. Who thinks about breathing?

He looked at the tower as he waited for the traffic light to turn from red to green. The red light way up there on the top of the tower pulsed like a heartbeat.

What is this big thing? He wondered. What does it do? What is that red light for? Is it also on during the day? He never noticed.

He looked left and right. No one else was out driving. Only him, Brian McKenna. No one else was awake. Only him at three o'clock in the morning. He felt like he owned the world. No police cars in sight, but he would never drive through that red traffic light. He would wait because his driver's license was still damp from birth. The Driver's Ed course he had taken during his junior year in high school, the year he had just finished, was still fresh in his mind. "Obey the law," his teacher had said. "Follow the rules. A good citizen drives safely."

He'd wait.

He looked again at the tower's light and smiled at the way it pulsed. Long John Nebel was talking about alien abductions on the Rambler American's AM radio. Brian McKenna looked at the tower's long legs and round, bulging body, so high up there. Such long legs. And so many of them. Like an enormous steel spider. Maybe this huge, silent thing was getting ready to roar and pull its feet up out of the ground and start smashing buildings. Maybe start the War of the Worlds. He chuckled inside the 10-year-old car he had gotten for the hundred bucks he had saved from his *Newsday* route.

"What *is* this thing? Why is it *here*?" he said.

No one heard him.

The traffic light turned green. Brian McKenna looked left and right. No one was there. He let out the clutch and turned right. He could have turned left, but he turned right. It didn't matter tonight. He'd start the new job - the one his mother had gotten for him - in two weeks. This two-hour drive was to practice waking early and staying awake. In just two weeks, school would be over and it would be summer, and he would work every night for Mr. Olson. That would be good. He'd make money working for Mr. Olson. He'd be able to help his mother.

"What *is* that thing?" he muttered, glancing one more time at the tower.

No one heard him.

Later that day, in Los Angeles, three bullets would strike Bobby Kennedy. One would graze his forehead; another would lodge harmlessly in his neck. The third bullet would crash through his skull behind his right ear and rip through his brain. He would die the next day at 1:44 A.M., Thursday, June 6, 1968.

The Milk

Ole Olson owned the milk route. The grass-green, Chevy C10, sidestep pickup had been his workhorse for the past two years and he was very pleased with it. He told Brian to get out and let down the tailgate so he could back the truck into the loading dock by his milk locker. Brian did as he was told. He was good that way.

Ole Olson slid out of the Chevy like a fat sack of old dungarees and huffed his way up the few concrete steps, with Brian following.

"First things first, young fella," Ole Olson said, pointing around at the dairy plant. "This is where the milk comes from. I don't own the dairy, just the route. I ain't no millionaire so don't get any ideas about hitting me on the head and robbing me in the dark." He knuckled his green baseball cap twice and chuckled.

Seventeen-year-old Brian McKenna smiled, nodded, but said nothing.

"I rent the milk locker from the rich guy that owns the dairy. Everything starts here. It's quiet now, but during the day this place is humming. They even used to milk the cows here, but no more."

"I remember that," Brian said.

"That's right. You grew up in this neighborhood, didn't you?" Ole Olson said. "I guess you *would* remember."

Brian nodded.

"Yeah, they got rid of the cows in Sixty or Sixty-one," Ole Olson said. "The owner, Mr. Sanderson, sold most of the property to the developers and now it's all houses except for these couple of acres he held onto to keep the plant going. He got rich on that property sale, and the plant workers got to keep their jobs. So did I. He's a smart fella, that Mr. Sanderson."

Brian nodded.

"So you got some memories of this place, eh?" Ole Olson said.

"Yes."

"What's your favorite?"

"Me and my friends used to feed the cows with the grass we got when we mowed the lawns," Brian said. "We'd put the grass in paper grocery bags we'd get from our mothers and we'd bring them here and throw them over the fence for the cows. They came running. It was fun to watch. All the kids did it."

"Well, to see those cows nowadays I suppose you'd have to go upstate," Ole Olson said. "The raw milk comes in by tractor trailers these days, but they still process it here. That's why it's so fresh. We have the best milk in the world."

Brian nodded, remembering the fresh smell of the grass and the lowing the cows made as they hurried over and nosed into the tossed brown bags.

"Okay, let's load 'er up," Ole Olson said, clapping his hands once. He keyed the padlock on the insulated wooden door, yanked it open with a grunt, and turned on the light. The milk was stacked across the back wall, five cases high, like brides waiting.

"One thing you can depend on is milk, young fella," Ole Olson said opening his arms, like he was expecting the white brides to step forward and hug him. "Open the door and there it is, night after night. Milk never fails and it never disappoints. It's always there for us."

Brian could see his breath. It was like going from summer to winter in an instant. He shivered.

"You'll get used to the cold," Ole Olson said. "And we're not in here that long. You'll see. The ice house is colder. I'll show you that in a few minutes."

A three-foot-long steel rod was leaning against the wall by the door. Ole grabbed it by its handle, took two steps, and snagged the bottom case with the hook at the end of the rod. He held the top case with his other hand and grunted as he slid the stack out the door and to the rear of the truck.

"Milkman's hand truck," he chuckled. "That's how we do it. Hey, hop in the back of the truck and load them up in rows, okay? Go five crates wide and three levels high. We're going to go back seven rows to the tailgate, but go three high before you move back to the next row, okay? There's an order to all of this. A method to my madness!" He chuckled.

"Okay," Brian said.

"That's good. You're a smart young fella. Now with the last row, the one by the tailgate, go just *two* high so we'll have room for the miscellaneous items.

"Okay."

"That's going to give us a hundred crates. One-thousand two-hundred beautiful quarts of fresh milk in clean, glass bottles. God, I love the look of fresh milk." He wrapped his arms around a stack and laughed. "You know what they say, young fella. You can't beat milk, but you can sure whip cream!"

Ole Olson laughed at his own joke. Brian thought about it for a moment; got it, and smiled.

"Whip cream," Brian said. "That's funny."

"Yep! That's an old milkman joke. I got a million of 'em!"

Brian smiled.

"Well, maybe not a *million*, but I got enough of them. You'll see."

"Okay," Brian said.

"Hey, I got a book I want you to read, young fella. It's called *How to Be a Milkman*, by Carey Bottles."

Brian stared at Ole Olson.

"Carey Bottles? Get it?"

"Oh!" Brian laughed.

"They get easier to understand once you've had your coffee," Ole Olson chuckled. "Okay, so how about you get these cases on our truck and I'll go get us another stack."

Brian McKenna nodded and did as he was told.

"That's good," Ole Olson said, breathing heavily when he slid out the third stack. "Now you come on over here and get the rest of these stacks out of the locker and load them up. You need to learn how to do all of this, young fella." He took a green washcloth out of his back pocket and mopped sweat off his brow. "Take your time, but not too much time. It's cold in there!" He chuckled. "Oh, and don't drop anything. I gotta pay for that milk if you drop it."

Brian nodded and went to work.

Ole Olson watched and nodded. "You're a quick study, young fella," he said. "I like that. Now go get the miscellaneous stuff. It's stacked on the left side."

"Miscellaneous stuff?" Brian said.

"The eggs, OJ, butter. All of that. It's in three cases. You can't miss them. Go on."

Brian did as he was told.

"You drive a stick, right?" Ole Olson said as Brian finished loading the truck. Brian nodded. "Good. Pull it up a few feet and then get out and close the tailgate. I'll get the locker door."

Brian moved the truck without jolting it. Ole Olson watched, nodded, and smiled. He walked down the steps. Brian got out of the truck, closed the tailgate, and moved to the passenger side.

"I like you, young fella. You're a good worker," Ole Olson said. "You're gonna make a great milkman. I can tell. One more thing you need to know before we go any further, though. There's a broom and shovel behind your seat."

Brian nodded.

"That's for broken glass," Ole Olson said. "If you ever get to drive this truck on your own and you cut a corner too close because you're in a hurry, you'll bump up onto the curb and spill glass. That's not good, young fella. And not just because of the noise and the mess it makes, but also because my name's on every bottle. Olson's Dairy. Everybody around here knows who I am. I'm one famous milkman, and if you ever leave a mess of busted glass in the street with *my* name on it for the cops to find, they'll be coming after *me*, not *you*. And once they come after me, *I'll* be coming after *you*, young fella. And if that ever happens, you'll wish *I* was the cops and not old Ole Olson." He waved a pudgy fist but Brian could see that he was smiling in the glow of the dashboard light, so he smiled back.

"I got it, Mr. Olson," he said. "I'll be real careful."

"You'd *better* be real careful, young fella, or you'll get my famous knuckle sandwich for lunch," Ole Olson laughed and waved his fat fist again. "And don't call me Mr. Olson. That was my father's name and he's long gone. We're going to be working together so call me Ole. We're just a couple of hard-working guys in this truck. We go with first names all the way, young fella."

"Okay, Ole," Brian said.

He drove to the far side of the loading dock, backed in, and slid out of the truck.

"C'mon, young fella. One more stop before we head out to the route. I'll introduce you to the wonders of the ice house and show you the proper way to shovel ice chips. This is a real important part of being a milkman."

It was the biggest pile of chipped ice Brian had ever seen and the machine kept grinding out more. Ice cascaded from a metal chute near the ceiling down onto the floor. It was like mechanical weather. Brian couldn't stop staring at it. It was much colder in here than it was in the milk locker. He shivered.

Ole Olson handed him the snow shovel. "Okay, best way to stop shivering is to start shoveling. Just pile that ice on the cases, front to back." Brian took the shovel and went to work. He picked up a sliver of ice and put it in his mouth. It tasted good, cold and clean.

"How high should I go?" Brian said.

"About a foot all the way across," Ole Olson said. "It's a warm night. That will be enough. We're lucky we're the first ones here. Get here too late and the other guys will have grabbed most of the ice. Then we'd have to hang around waiting for the machine to catch up with us. That's not good. It wastes too much time. We gotta move, move, move when we're on the routes, and we gotta watch out for Fabrizio. He's the milk inspector from the Board of Health. I'll tell you more about him later."

Brian nodded and did as he was told.

They pulled out of the dairy's lot and drove a half mile to the diner, which never closed, not even on Christmas.

"Time for breakfast," Ole Olson said. "I'll go get it. My treat. That's part of the deal. We'll eat in the truck on our way to our first stop. That saves time. I like to start the day with a big greasy hamburger on a Kaiser roll, with lots of fried onions and ketchup. Oh and salt and pepper, too. And I like it rare. I want my breakfast to moo when I bite into it. Yep, that's the best breakfast in the world. Keeps a man going, and in more ways than one." He chuckled. "What do you want for breakfast, young fella?"

"Um, I like apple turnovers?" Brian said.

"How many? Four? Five?"

"Just one," Brian said. "That's all I need. Just one. Thanks, Ole."

"Just *one*? Well, to each his own," Ole Olson said. "That's not much of a breakfast, but you'll learn. I'm sure you will. Want a coffee?"

"Sure."

"I'll get you a big one. How do you take it?"

"Black, no sugar."

"That's disgusting. I'm a light-and-sweet man myself," Ole Olson said. "Four sugars and plenty of cream. But to each his own, right?"

"I guess so. Thanks, Ole," Brian said. He hadn't thought to bring any money with him. He didn't have much money anyway. That's why he needed this job.

"Part of the deal, young fella. Part of the deal. Boss buys the breakfast. And *I'm* the boss. Don't you ever forget that," he chuckled.

"I won't," Brian said.

"But you have to learn how to eat the right things at the right time if you're gonna be a strong milkman, young fella," Ole Olson said as he grabbed the doorframe and grunted off the bench seat. "Maybe you'll try my special burger one of these nights. It's *real* good."

Brian nodded.

"That's good. You should pay attention to what I'm teaching you, young fella. I have a *lot* to teach you."

"Okay," Brian said, nodding again. Three times.

"Now stay in the truck and watch the milk. Don't let anybody mess with the milk. I'll be right back." He waddled toward the diner.

"Okay," Brian said to himself.

The coffee smelled wonderful in the truck's cab. Brian lifted the cap and blew on it. It was too hot to drink.

"Don't burn yourself," Ole Olson said.

Brian nodded and put the cap back on the paper cup.

Ole Olson shifted gears with his hamburger hand and talked with his mouth full.

"Lef's talk 'bot somfing important," he said before swallowing.

"Okay," Brian said.

"Let's talk about *women*. Do you want to know what I'm gonna buy when I get rich, young fella? And I *will* get rich," he said, waving the hamburger. "You want to know *why* I'll get rich?"

Brian shrugged.

"I'll get rich because *everyone* needs milk," Ole Olson said. "And milkmen will *always* have work because people don't like to go to the store for milk. Milk is one of life's essential things and it's best served in a clear-glass bottle with a paper cap. These fancy new grocery stores that are opening up all over the place don't have the glass bottles. We do. These fancy new grocery stores are big, but they only sell milk in those lousy cardboard containers. You seen those? They got this wax on the insides and the outsides. That's no way to serve milk. That wax and that cardboard affect the taste of the milk and it can even give you the cancer. I read about that somewhere, I forget where, but it's the god's truth. You can take it to the bank, young fella. No one is ever gonna buy milk from these fancy new grocery stores. It's just not as good as *our* milk. Mark my words on that." He smacked the steering wheel with the flat of his hand and laughed. "We're both gonna get rich selling milk in clean glass bottles with fresh paper caps because some things in this life are just never gonna change. Stick around long enough and you'll see what I mean, young fella."

"Okay," Brian said, nodding.

"So do you really want to know what I'm going to buy when I'm rich?" Ole Olsson said, smiling and taking another bite of his burger.

"I do. I mean, I *guess* I do," Brian said. "Um. Okay."

"I'm gonna buy roomful of *tifs*," Ole Olson said through a wad of hamburger. He swallowed and laughed.

"Yeah, a big roomful of *boobies* so I can take off my shirt and trousers and roll around in them after work." Ole Olson wiggled his girth on the bench seat and laughed. He bounced in the seat four times and stroked the steering wheel from top to sides and back again. "WOO! WOO! YEAH! A big roomful of *boobies*! That's my dream, young fella. My *dream!*" Ole Olson smiled at Brian. "You understand, right?" he said. "I mean, what guy wouldn't want to have a roomful of boobies?"

Brian quivered a nervous smile at the windshield and shrugged.

"So what do you think, young fella?" Ole Olson said.

"Um, about what?" Brian said.

"The boobies! My plan! My dream!" Ole Olson shouted. "My big, beautiful roomful of boobies!"

"Um. I don't know," Brian said, embarrassed.

"You don't *know*?"

"Um, no. I don't know," Brian said. "How would you even *do* that? They're part of the woman's body. How could you just have. . . *those*?"

"The boobies? Just the boobies? Use your imagination, young fella. A roomful of fluffy boobies in all sizes and colors. Big ones, small ones, all of them like soft throw pillows. You know what a throw pillow is, don't you?" Brian nodded. "Good. Think of them that way. Fluffy and soft. Big and small. Boobies everywhere. Across the floor, up the walls, stuck to the ceiling like helium balloons. Everywhere! It's perfect. Use your imagination. It's my *dream!*"

"Um, okay," Brian said.

"You kids. You just don't understand dreams. That's what matters in life, you know. Dreams!" Ole Olson laughed, shook his big head. "You kids." He stuffed the rest of the burger into his mouth. Chewed. Chuckled. Licked his fingers.

Brian blushed and looked out at the Long Island Expressway sliding away under the truck.

"Our first of two-hundred stops will be the Einbinder residence," Ole Olson said as they entered the neighborhood. "And I say *residence* because this is one fancy area. You'd know that if you saw it during the day. You'd also know that Myra

Einbinder is a pain in the rear end, but you won't get to meet her because she'll never be awake when we're on our route. You're lucky you don't have to try to collect money from her. She's tighter than a cat's kiester and she won't leave the money in the milk box. She says the neighborhood is filled with thieves, but look around you, young fella. You see any thieves here? It's the middle of the night. You see any thieves? You see any *people* besides us? We're the only people awake in the whole world right now, young fella. We're the *milkmen*. The only thieves around here live *in* these houses. Believe me. I have to go collect from her in person, and she doesn't like to pay. She's always surprised when I show up, even though I call her first to say I'm on my way. People can be creepy, young fella, especially the rich ones. They're the worst. Always remember that. And *always* get paid. You'll learn that in life, and I'm a good teacher when it comes to that. Believe me, okay?"

"Okay," Brian said.

"So here we are," Ole Olson said, backing into the block. He did this because Brian had to deliver to all the houses that were on the passenger side of the truck. Ole Olson did the houses that were on the driver's side, but there were *far* fewer of those because of the way Ole Olson drove the route when he had a helper. "I'm not gonna pay a kid fifteen bucks a night to watch *me* deliver milk," he had told his wife, Mae. "I'll back into the streets so he gets just about all of the stops. I'm the boss so I get to do that. Hey, make me a sandwich while you're up, will ya? I need a snack."

Mae got up and made him a sandwich. She said nothing.

"Myra Einbinder gets four bottles of whole milk," Ole Olson said. "Her milk box is on the front stoop. Right there. See it? It's right there. See it?" Brian nodded. "Good. Okay, take your flashlight and go. And be fast. We don't have all night. Well, actually we *do* have all night," he chuckled. "But let's see if we can get home early today, okay? And remember to take the milk from the next to the last row *first*. The last row has the miscellaneous stuff on top. We'll move that stuff around later. And use the sidestep to roll the quilt back over the milk when you put the empties in the case. That way the ice won't melt too fast. Ice is life in the milkman business, and we gotta watch out for Fabrizio, the milk inspector. Always remember that, young fella. Fabrizio's on the prowl. That man never sleeps."

"Okay," Brian said.

"Good," Ole Olson said. "Go!"

Brian moved, 17-year-old-fast. Ole Olson watched through the rear window. He gave Brian a thumbs up. Brian smiled and pulled four quarts of whole milk from the ice and put them into the aluminum, eight-bottle carrier. The ice dropped through the spaces and down onto the bottles on the lower level. It made a sad sound, like coins going down the sewer.

"I have a question," Brian said a half-hour later.

"Shoot," Ole Olson said.

"Where do milkmen go to pee?" Brian whispered.

"Do you need to pee?"

Brian squirmed, embarrassed.

"You do, don't you?"

He nodded.

"Ah, black coffee will do that to you. Goes right through you. It's worse than beer," Ole Olson said, pulling to the curb.

"Okay, go in the back and get an empty," he said. "Then come back here."

Brian slipped out of the truck and did as he was told.

"Stand in the street with the door half-open to hide your weenie. Then pee in the bottle," Ole Olson said. "Go ahead. It's okay. And if you tell me you need a bottle with a wider opening I'm gonna to be jealous." He chuckled.

"Really? Just pee in the bottle?" Brian said.

"Yes, and make it snappy. I won't look," Ole Olson said.

"But the milk goes in there," Brian said.

"So does the pee. That's one of the Milkman Rules. The guys at the plant know we all do this and they sterilize the bottles real good. Don't worry. Just go. Hurry up."

Brian did as he was told.

"What do I do with the bottle?" he said holding it up.

"Wow, you nearly filled 'er up!"

"I really had to go," Brian said.

"Put the bottle in one of the cases," Ole Olson said. "It's okay. That's how we do it. We'll dump the pee back at the plant. Never dump it in the street. It stinks. And be sure you don't deliver it." He chuckled. "It ain't lemonade."

Brian did as he was told.

"Ole?" Brian said three stops later.

"Yep."

"What do I do if I have to poop?"

"Well, you'd better squint your eyes tight and aim real good, young fella," Ole Olson laughed. "There's just so much room in a milk bottle."

Brian returned from delivering eight quarts of whole milk to the back stoop of a split-level house in Plainview when he saw Ole Olson and a smaller man standing next to the Chevy. They were both watching the needle on a thermometer that the smaller man had stabbed through the paper cap of a random milk bottle. It was 7:00 AM and there wasn't much ice left on the milk. The man was smiling. Ole Olson wasn't.

Brian stood on the sidewalk next to what must have been the man's Ford Fairlane and watched. He said nothing. Ole Olson had told him a story about Mario Fabrizio. Could this be him?

The thermometer's needle stopped moving downward.

"Son of a bitch," Mario Fabrizio muttered, putting the bottle back into the case. "Don't deliver that one. It's cold enough, but just barely. You got lucky today, Olson, but your luck's not going to last long in *this* heat. I'll see you around." He got into the Fairlane, turned on his left blinker, even though no one else was on the road, and drove off.

"Good thing he didn't see the pee bottle," Ole Olson said.

Brian nodded as he watched the Fairlane go.

"Sorry, Ole."

"Don't be. When you gotta go, you gotta go. I'm no different. We're only human."

They finished the route with cautious speed, looking around each corner for Mario Fabrizio. They didn't see him again that day.

"We got lucky today, young fella," Ole Olson said. "Fabrizio doesn't give warnings and it's a good thing we iced the load well because if that guy radios in for a tow truck, it's game over."

Brian nodded but said nothing.

"Let's make double-sure we ice it up high tonight. It's going to be another scorcher. Remind me, okay?"

"Okay, Ole."

"And we'll move fast. No dawdling."

"We won't, Ole."

"Good," Ole Olson said. "It's you and me against that guy. And he never stops prowling. He's like a zombie. I'd love to give him my famous knuckle sandwich for lunch one of these days." He shook his fist.

"Yes," Brian said.

"You and me, young fella. You and me." Ole Olson opened his fist and patted Brian on his knee. "You and me."

"Do you know what that is, Ole?" Brian had said at four in the morning on that first night. He pointed at the water tower.

"What?" Ole Olson said.

"That," Brian said, pointing.

Ole Olson followed Brian's finger. "The water tower?" he said. "You don't know what that is?"

"No," Brian said.

"It's a water tower," Ole Olson laughed. "It's where the water comes from. Smile and tell me you're kidding. You're kidding, right? You don't know what a water tower is? *Really?*"

"No, I don't. What does it do?"

"How could you not know?" Ole Olson said.

"No one ever told me what it is," Brian said. "What does it do? How does it work?"

"What does it *do*? It holds the water for all of us. It's where we get our drinking water, the water for our showers, all the water we use for *everything*. It comes from up there." Ole Olson pointed. "Water towers are all over the place on Long Island. You don't know that? Jeez."

"But how does it *work*?" Brian said.

35

Ole Olson chuckled. "Oh, *that's* what you want to know? Well, they got these big pumps. They're in a building at the bottom of the tower. You'll see the building when we drive by. I'll point it out to you. The water is in the ground in what they call the aquifer. It's like a big lake, only underground. All of Long Island gets its water from that big lake. Get it?"

"It's underground?"

"Yes," Ole Olson said.

Brian nodded, but he found it hard to believe that there was a lake under the ground. Wouldn't it just fill up with dirt? How could the water be so clean if it had all that dirt in it?

"How do the pumps work?" Brian said.

"The pumps suck the water up like a straw and pump it way up there into the top of the tank. From there, the water just flows by gravity through the pipes under the streets that connect the tower to our houses. It works the same way water flowing down a mountain works. You know what gravity is, don't you?"

"Yes."

"What it is?"

"Um, it's what makes stuff fall?" Brian said.

"That's right, and the height of the tower is what gives the water its pressure. The higher the tower, the higher the water pressure. Without those towers, the water would just dribble out of our faucets. You'd get a lousy shower after working all night. You don't want a lousy shower, do you?"

"No," Brian said.

"You really don't know any of this, do you?"

"No," Brian said.

"Jeez, you kids are pretty stupid nowadays," Ole Olson said.

"I guess so," Brian shrugged.

"Don't they teach you this stuff in school?"

"No," Brian said.

"What *do* they teach you in school these days?" Ole Olson said.

"Other stuff. Useless stuff," Brian said.

"Do you read the newspapers?"

"No. We can't afford newspapers, and my mother says there's nothing but bad news in there anyway and reading about it would just make us sad."

"Do you watch the news on the TV?" Ole Olson said.

"No."

"Same reason?"

"Yes," Brian said.

"All the more reason why we should talk about a roomful of boobies. There's nothing happier than that. Besides, the night is long and we gotta talk about *something*. Might as well be boobies. Hey, there's the building with the pumps. See it?" He pointed.

Brian nodded, but said nothing.

What if it's God? Brian wondered the following April when he was doing the route by himself and staring at the red light on top of the tower as he waited for the traffic light to turn green. He wasn't sure if he believed in God. What if that red light up there on the tower is watching over me? Is that why it's way up there? So it can see me on the whole route? What if that red light is really God? Is he protecting me? And if he is, why didn't he protect Sean? Do they have red lights on towers in Vietnam?

He was 52 deliveries into Route 1. One-hundred forty-eight deliveries to go. The quilt was tucked tightly across the cases and the ice was in good shape. And it was a cool night. There will be no problem with Fabrizio on this night. Brian was getting better at this and he knew it. And he wouldn't have to go into the Marines like Sean did. He could do the milk and help his mother. He didn't have to die like Sean did. He could do the milk forever. There will always be milkmen. Nothing will ever change that. He knew this was true because Ole Olson had told him so.

Brian discovered Long John Nebel on the radio before he started driving the route, way back when he had been practicing to stay awake. That was last summer. It seemed so long ago. Ole Olson didn't listen to the radio. He preferred to talk, and mostly nonstop about what he had done with women when he was in the Navy. Brian wasn't sure whether any of those stories were true. Ole Olson wasn't a very handsome man, and the stories he told were both outrageous and acrobatic, and Ole Olson was no acrobat.

But maybe Ole Olson was in better shape and handsome when he was in the Navy. He said that he was a cook on a big ship, and because of that, he didn't like to cook now. He just liked to eat. At first, Brian thought that maybe that was how Ole Olson had gotten so fat. He must have tasted all that food as he cooked for the thousands of sailors. But then, Ole Olson told Brian what he had for dinner each day. He said it was to give him the energy he needed to work the route.

"Everybody else's breakfast time is my dinner time because I work nights," Ole Olson had said. "You'll get just like me when it comes to that. I mean the time thing. You'll see. Time is all reversed for us."

Brian nodded.

"Anyway, when I get home, my dinner is a box of Frosted Flakes. I have this big metal bowl. It's really a salad bowl for when me and Mae have company over for dinner, which isn't often, so I use the bowl for the cereal. And that's okay because I make my own rules. You should, too. That's what men do. We make our own rules. That's why I'm in my own business. So I can make my own rules. If I want eat cereal from a salad bowl then that's just what I'm gonna do. You agree, right?"

Brian nodded.

"Good. That's good that you agree with me. Anyway, then I pour a big can of fruit cocktail into the bowl. I never drain the syrup. It just goes right onto the Frosted Flakes. Mmmm. The syrup is the best part, and it's healthy to eat fruit. You can read up on that if you want to. Just go to the library."

"Okay," Brian said.

"And to all of that good stuff I add a pint of half-and-half, and a quart of whole milk. Sometimes I'll also add some heavy cream. It depends on the day and my mood. You understand?"

"Yes," Brian said.

"Anyway, that gets me through to lunch, which I eat around four o'clock in the afternoon. I like to eat a half-dozen fried eggs and a half-pound of bacon for lunch. It's all protein and protein gives you energy. Mae cooks the bacon first and then she fries the eggs in the bacon fat. It's the best. Oh, and I have three Thomas' English muffins with Smuckers grape jelly and Land-O-Lakes butter, the same stuff we deliver. It's the best."

"And after lunch I go to sleep. At six o'clock. *Always* at six o'clock. That's important."

Brian nodded.

"I have my breakfast from the diner before we start the route," Ole Olson went on. "But you know that now, don't you, young fella? You really should try the hamburger. Apple turnovers will put the pounds on you. And always have a thick-shake float from Carvel at some point during the day if you can.

Those shakes put the meat on your bones. You're too skinny. Try the chocolate one. Mmmm."

"Okay," Brian said, wishing he could listen to the radio.

Long John Nebel had been on WOR AM radio from the mid-'50s until WNBC AM hired him away from WOR AM in 1962 for the incredible salary of $100,000 a year. He talked all night long, and mostly about UFOs, voodoo, witchcraft, parapsychology, conspiracy theories, and ghosts. No-Doz caffeine pills sponsored the show but Brian didn't use those. All he needed to stay up all night was that first cup of black coffee from the diner.

Brian listened to Long John because there wasn't much else on the radio in the middle of the night, and the chat about all those strange things in the world captured his imagination. He was on the route by himself now. He ran to the milk boxes and got back into the cab as quickly as possible so he wouldn't miss too much Long John. This made him a very good milkman, but he would sometimes have to drive back to a few houses on the route to make sure he had actually delivered the milk. There's monotony to delivering milk, and monotony can lead to mistakes, so he went back and checked the boxes. He needed this job.

Half of Ole Olson's 400 or so customers got a delivery on Monday, Wednesday, and Friday mornings. The other half got their deliveries on Tuesday, Thursday, and Saturday mornings. Saturday night was the one night off. Ole Olson thought of it as date night. He and Mae would go out to dinner and a movie, and then sleep in on Sunday. He'd stay up a bit later on Sunday, but then it would start all over again at 2 AM on Monday morning. That was the milkman's life.

When Brian started as Ole Olson's helper he couldn't believe how Ole Olson knew how to get from one house to the next, let alone how he knew how to back into streets so that most of the delivery work fell on Brian's side of the truck.

"How do you remember all of this?" he said on that first night.

"I just do," Ole Olson said. "You'll get like me, too. You'll see."

"But how did you learn?"

"It's all in the book," Ole Olson said, laying his right hand on the route book that was on the bench seat between them. "I'll show you when we make the next stop. That's going to be on your side of the truck, by the way," he chuckled.

Brian smiled. He liked getting in and out of the truck, especially on a warm night like this one was.

He ran the four quarts of skim milk up to the galvanized milk box on the front stoop, grabbed the empties and the envelope with the money, and then ran back to the truck. He hopped up on the sidestep to place the empties into the case from which he had just taken the four bottles of skim. When the case was filled with empties, he knew Ole Olson would tell him what to do with it. Brian tried to imagine what that would be. Moving the cases around in the truck without disrupting the ice was like solving one of those slide puzzles where you have to thumb all the plastic tiles into numerical order.

He got back in the truck and handed the money envelope to Ole Olson, who put it into the route book on that customer's page.

"Okay, here's how it works, young fella. You see this here?" Ole Olson said pointing at a series of letters and numbers at the top of the page. Brian nodded. "Read it."

"L, R. XRR, R, 2L, 4R, FS," Brian said. "What does it mean?"

"It's code," Ole Olson said. "It tells us how we get to the next stop."

"How does it work?"

"I'll start driving. You give me the letters as I do," Ole Olson said.

"Okay," Brian said.

Ole Olson let out the clutch and they rolled slowly down the street "What's the first letter," he said, already knowing it by heart.

Brian looked down with his flashlight. "L," he said.

"Good." Ole Olson drove to the corner and turned left. "L means left. So we turn left." He did. "What's next?"

"R."

"We turn right at the next corner. Get it?"

"Yes."

"What's next?" Ole Olson said as they approached a railroad crossing. The gates were up.

"XRR."

"Cross the railroad tracks," Ole Olson said. "Get it?"

"Yes."

What's next?"

"R."

"Right turn," Ole Olson said. "What's next?"

"Two L," Brian said.

"Second left turn."

"I see," Brian said.

"And next?"

"Four R," Brian said.

"That's the next to the last one, right?" Ole Olson said.

"Yes."

"The next-to-last one is always the position of the house on the block. The house we need is four R, the fourth house on the right. We do it this way because most of the time you can't see the house numbers, and we don't want to be waving our flashlights at people's houses. We're liable to wake them up and we can't have that. We have to be respectful of their sleep. Okay, what's last in the code?"

Brian looked down.

"FS," he said.

"That stands for front stoop. It's where you'll find the milk box. If the box was in the back of the house it would read BS. That stands for back stoop, not the other kind of BS. You can save *that* kind of BS for when you need a name for what they're teaching you in that school of yours."

"You got that right," Brian said. "And this code is so *simple*."

"It is once you understand it, and I'm a good teacher," Ole Olson said. "But if I add a customer to the route, I have to make darn sure I fix the directions before and after that new customer in the book. If I forget to do that, we're both going to get lost out here in the dark."

Brian nodded.

"You're going to be a great milkman, young fella," Ole Olson said. "Now look over here in the route book. This is where it shows us what this customer is getting today. Today is Monday, so let's look."

Brian looked. It read 2W. 2S. 1OJ. Ole Olson pointed at each set of numbers and letters. "Okay two-W is two whole milk; two-S is two skim milk. Somebody must be on a diet." He grabbed his belly and chuckled. "And then they get one quart of orange juice. They get the same thing every Monday unless they leave a note in the box to change it. Okay, young fella, go give to them."

Brian moved quickly.

"What about the other miscellaneous stuff?" he said when he was back in the truck.

"Well, AC is apple cider. That's popular in the fall. EG is eggnog. We'll sell a lot of that around the holidays. BM is buttermilk, not bowel movement." He chuckled. "Two half-signs is Half and Half. HC is heavy cream. B is butter. You'll get used to it. It's easy to figure it all out. And if you're good enough for me to let you loose on the route by yourself someday you'll know as much as I do about it. Well, maybe not *as* much, but enough." He let loose a belly laugh.

They finished the route at 8 AM that first morning and unloaded the empties onto the loading dock at the dairy. "We just stack them here for the guys," Ole Olson said. "They'll put them through the sterilizer and refill them with milk. Later this afternoon, they'll load our order for tomorrow in our milk locker. We rent that locker from the dairy, the same as every other milkman working out of here. And we keep out of each other's way. We never try to steal each other's customers. Always remember that. That's the Milkman's Creed. We all respect each other's routes. It's how we all survive. There will always be milkmen, young fella. Don't you ever forget that. Your future is secure now. You can take that to the bank. Now, go run the pee bottles over to the toilet. It's right there. See it?"

Brian nodded and did as he was told.

"Everything we need will be here for us tonight when we get ready to do the other route, the one you and your mother are on," Ole Olson said when Brian came back with the empties. "There are two routes. We call the one we just did Route 1, and the other is Route 2 to keep it simple. I could have called them Laurel and Hardy, or Abbott and Costello, but I like to keep things simple," he chuckled. "Each has about two-hundred houses. It usually takes six hours, start to finish, unless the weather is real bad."

"Okay," Brian said.

"So now we get you home," Ole Olson said. "Put those empties with the others and hop in."

Brian did as he was told.

Ole Olson pulled to the curb in front of Brian's house.

He reached into his pocket and took out a roll of bills. He counted out 15 singles. "Your pay for the night, young fella. Not bad for six hours of work, is it? No, it ain't. And no taxes to pay. We'll keep that between us guys."

Brian sat looking at the pile of singles in his hands. He had never made so much money in such a short amount of time. And he had had so much fun doing it. He wanted to do this job forever.

Ole Olson watched Brian and smiled.

"It's a good feeling, isn't it?" he said.

Brian nodded and then turned and smiled.

"Thanks, Ole."

"You earned every penny of it, young fella."

Brian smiled and started to get out of the truck.

"Hang on," Ole Olson said, looking down at Brian's old sneakers. He reached back into the wad of bills and counted out another ten singles. He held them out to Brian. "Here," he said. "Take this."

"What for?" Brian said, afraid to touch the money.

"For a better pair of shoes. I want you to go to Goldman Brothers later on this morning. They have good work shoes there. You can get a strong pair for ten bucks. A milkman needs good, strong shoes. Those sneakers won't be any good when the weather gets cold, and I don't want you getting hurt. I need you, Brian. Get used to wearing better shoes now and you'll be okay when it snows."

"Gosh. Thanks, Ole." Brian took the singles.

"Don't mention it, Brian, and don't oversleep. I'll be by to pick you up at 2 AM. Make sure you're up, dressed, and ready to go. Sit on your stoop. The weather's supposed to be okay tomorrow. No rain. And, hey, maybe you'll even try one of my special hamburgers with the greasy onions." He chuckled.

"Okay, Ole," Brian said. "Thanks."

"Now go take a shower. Get some good food in you, and then go out and buy those work shoes at Goldman's. Stay up until six o'clock tonight and then hit the rack. No staying up to watch TV. A young milkman like you needs his sleep." He waggled his index finger. "And don't forget to set your alarm."

"Okay, Ole," Brian said.

He did as he was told. He was good that way. And while he was showering that morning, he thought about the warm water that was falling onto him from that high water tower. It fell because of gravity. He knew that now. And there was a big lake under the ground. Ole Olson had taught him that, too. It felt good to know things, and Ole Olson was a great teacher.

And then he wondered how the water got hot.

Maybe he'd ask about that tonight.

Hannah

Fourteen-year-old Hannah Kepler stared at her scuffed shoes as she waited on the sidewalk for the school bus. Her shoulder-length, black hair hung over her cheeks, brushing against the minor acne that her mother kept telling her to wash.

"What's Olive Oyl doing?" Cathy whispered to Patty, not wanting to turn around. They were about 20 feet down the block from Hannah.

"What she always does," Patty whispered, looking past Cathy at Hannah. "Counting her big feet."

"Are there still just two of them?" Cathy giggled.

"Yes, like two canoes, but she's so stupid she has to keep counting them," Patty said.

Cathy glanced around quickly and turned back. "She's such a retard," she whispered.

"The worst," Patty agreed.

At five-foot 11-inches tall, Hannah Kepler was the tallest girl in school. She weighed just 110 pound no matter how much she ate, which also made her the thinnest girl in school. That's why the mean kids called her Olive Oyl.

When Hannah was eight years old, she had to wear a brace to correct the curvature of her spine caused by a mild case of scoliosis. She was tall for her age even then, and because of the scoliosis, some of the grammar school kids called her Hannah Banana.

But then a few years later, she shot up with a sudden growth spurt and became Olive Oyl. The meaner kids, and Hannah's school had no shortage of those, called her that to her face. Hannah never acknowledged them when they did this, and that just made them bolder.

"Hey, Olive. Where's Popeye?" they'd sneer as she passed them in the hallway on her way to class. "How's Bluto doing? You eat your spinach today, Olive Oyl?"

Hannah seethed at this, but she said nothing.

She glanced down the block, with her widely spaced, piercingly blue eyes. No bus yet.

"Look at how *skinny* she is," Patty said. "Like a string bean. Yuck!"

"Yeah, or Olive Oyl," Cathy giggled. "That's such a great name for her. She is *so* ugly. Even Tommy said that to me the other day. He said he wouldn't touch her with a stick. He said she has cooties."

"She better not turn her head sideways," Patty said, watching Hannah look for the bus. "If the wind catches that nose she's going to take off like a kite."

Cathy giggled.

Hannah had a pronounced nose, like Barbra Streisand's, but that didn't bother Hannah. A nose is for smelling things, and Hannah's worked just fine. Besides, Barbra Streisand was beautiful.

The acne annoyed Hannah, but only because her mother wouldn't leave her alone about it. She kept asking Hannah why the other girls had clear skin and she didn't. She said Hannah's skin was embarrassing her. "People stare at you when we go to the store," her mother would say. "Don't you see them staring at you? Why don't you do something about your skin? Why don't you wash your face more?"

Hannah ignored her.

Hannah's teeth were small, straight, and very white, like baby teeth that had never fallen out. Her fingers were long and slender, like a pianist's. She didn't smile much, but when she did, her eyes grew larger and somehow bluer, and anyone who took the time to notice this knew that there was an exquisite beauty in Hannah that would someday blossom.

But no one ever said that to her.

She hugged her books to her flat chest and stepped back as the bus arrived. The driver pulled up to where the six kids were standing, which was about the length of the bus from where Hannah waited alone. She didn't move until all six of them climbed into the bus. Only then did she walk toward the steps. Hannah was not one to wait in lines.

"Good morning," the bus driver said.

"Good morning, Mr. Tate," Hannah said. "Thank you for taking me to school."

"You're welcome."

The other kids placed their books on the empty seats next to them as she passed by. Hannah didn't want to sit next to them either. She found an empty seat in the next-to-the-last row, behind where Cathy and Patty were sitting. They whispered to each other as she went by and slid into the seat.

The bus picked up speed as it moved down the street. Hannah reached into her left jacket pocket and took out the small bran muffin she had brought from home. She put the whole

49

muffin into her mouth and chewed it into a wet mush. She used her tongue to move the mush between her small teeth and her cheeks, being careful not to swallow any of it.

Her slender fingers then went into her right jacket pocket and withdrew a small, white envelope. She opened it and used her index finger and thumb to pinch the black pepper she had taken from home that morning. She raised this to her nose and snorted it, being sure not to swallow the bran muffin.

The sneeze was sudden and explosive. She formed her lips into an O as it arrived, leaning forward and down toward the two girls in front of her. Spittle and soggy bits of bran muffin, which could have been *anything*, splattered the backs of Cathy's and Patty's pretty hair and the flawless skin on their white necks. Both girls let loose a screech that caused Mr. Tate to stop the bus.

"What's going on back there?" he said into the rearview mirror. All the kids on the bus turned to see.

"I sneezed," Hannah said. "I have a bad cold. It could be the flu. Or pneumonia. She sneezed again, this time hitting both girls flush in their faces."

"Oh my *god*!" Cathy shouted clawing at her face. "You're *disgusting*! I need tissues!"

"I hope you die!" Patty screamed.

Mr. Tate jumped out of his seat and hurried back.

"Now, girls, stop that. She can't help it if she's sick."

"She's *disgusting*!" Cathy said. "Look at her pimples. She sprayed pimple juice and brown snot all over me. Gross!"

"It's not nice to speak of others in that way," Mr. Tate said to the two girls. "She's ill. It was an accident. Please show some kindness."

"Sorry," Hannah said, small white teeth exposed, a gleam in her blue eyes.

"There, she said she was sorry," Mr. Tate said. "Be nice."

"She has *cooties*!" Cathy screamed.

"Now stop that," Mr. Tate said. "Stop that right now."

The other kids were all kneeling backwards on their seats, watching and waiting for what might come next. Would there be a catfight? Hanna was so tall. Who would win?

"I hope you die, *pizza face*!" Cathy hissed. *"Die!"*

Hannah sneezed again.

Bullseye.

"Sorry," she whispered.

Tiny smile.

Klaus

"Do you ever drop your hamburger when you're driving?" Brian said as they pulled away from the diner.

"Not once," Ole Olson said. "I do drop some onions onto my belly from time to time. I eat them when I stop. You know, before I get out of the truck? I think of them as dessert." He let loose a belch and shifted with his burger hand. "Excuse me," he chuckled. "I meant to throw up."

Brian smiled as they got onto the Long Island Expressway. The only other drivers at that hour were probably drunks.

"What do you think would be the toughest food to eat while driving?" Brian said as he bit into his apple turnover. Ole Olson looked in his side mirror and merged.

"Hmm, let's see. The toughest food to eat while driving. Hmm." Ole Olson bit into his burger. "I supofe a lobda," he garbled.

"Yeah, a lobster would be real tough to eat while driving," Brian laughed, imagining Ole Olson trying to crack a claw by smashing it onto the gear shift's knob.

Ole Olson chewed, thought, and swallowed. "Or how about French onion soup?" he said, letting loose another wet belch. "The crock is real hot when you get it, and there's all that melted cheese hanging onto that big floating crouton. And that cheese is baked onto the sides of the crock. You gotta pick that off and eat it, too. It's the best part. Yum! But all that would be tough to eat while driving. You'd need four hands for French onion soup."

"Yeah," Brian said. "How about lasagna?"

"Cold or hot?" Ole Olson said.

"You can eat lasagna cold?" Brian said.

"You can eat *anything* cold, young fella. Always remember that. *Anything.*"

"Frozen TV dinners?" Brian said.

"It would be tough on the teeth, but you could do it. I'd rather not try it while driving, though. You don't want to get that aluminum foil anywhere near your fillings. It sets up some sort of radio wave that connects with lightning bolts or something. Hurts a lot. They teach you about that in school?"

"No," Brian said. "I learned that on my own."

"Me, too," Ole Olson said. "Some things are best learned the hard way, young fella."

Brian said nothing.

"Why do you drive this truck and not a milk truck?" Brian said a mile later.

"This *is* a milk truck," Ole Olson said. "We use it to deliver milk. That makes it a milk truck. Gosh, kids your age are dopey sometimes."

"No, Ole. I mean the boxy ones. The trucks that some of the other guys drive."

"Oh, you mean the Divcos," Ole Olson said.

"I don't know what that is," Brian said.

"Right, they don't teach you that in school, do they? The boxy trucks are Divcos."

"Dipcos?" Brian said.

54

"No, *Divco*, with a V. It's an old-school delivery truck. The name is an abbreviation of the name of the company that makes them. Detroit Industrial Vehicle Company. D-I-V-C-O. Divco. You're lucky we have the Chevy, though. Divcos are the worst."

"Why?" Brian said.

"Well, first of all, they're slower than a Chevy, so you can't take them on the Expressway. And a slow truck means our routes would take longer to finish. That means too much ice might melt in the summer and Fabrizio would be all over us. Not good. Oh, and that melting ice rots holes in the floor. Also not good. And they're much colder inside during the winter because the doors don't shut very well. They also have lousy heaters. I hate the cold."

Brian nodded, taking it all in.

"Let's see, what else? Okay, Divcos have two side mirrors but no rearview mirror. So we wouldn't be able to see out the back of the truck when we were backing up. Guys who drive Divcos bang into a lot of things when they back up. We don't need to bang into a lot of things. It's bad for business."

"They look like they're fun to drive, though," Brian said.

"Oh, yeah, you think so?" Ole Olson said, looking over at Brian. "Fun? You like driving a bucket of bolts standing up?"

"Some of the guys sit," Brian said. "I've seen them."

"Yeah, but both seats lift out, and those seats get in the way when you're delivering by yourself with a Divco. A lot of the guys remove the seats when they get to the first stop on their route. They stow them on top of the milk. They want to get out of either side of the truck, and fast. That's why they take out the seats. Divcos are set up to let the driver turn around, grab the milk, and jump out either way. But the guys who drive standing up have to be acrobats. And *young* acrobats."

"What do you mean?" Brian said.

"Well, a Divco is standard shift. So is this Chevy C10. But when you're driving while standing up, you have to work the gas with your right foot, and the other pedal, which is both the clutch *and* the brake, with your left foot."

"How can one pedal be both things?" Brian said.

"You push it half-way down to clutch. You push it the rest of the way down to brake," Ole Olson said. "So imagine you're going down the road at about 30 miles per hour, which is about all a Divco can do. The doors are wide open on both sides. You're standing up. There are no seatbelts because there are no seats. There's nothing but your two hands to hold you inside the Divco. It's rattling like mad, and you have all that milk right behind you. The only thing holding that milk in place is gravity."

"Okay," Brian said.

"So now you need to shift," Ole Olson said. "You have to let up on the gas to do that, but you're standing up, so that means you have to lean back on your right heel. With me so far?"

"Yes."

"Okay, so now your left foot goes onto the clutch, which is also the brake. You push it halfway down and shift with your right hand. You're steering with just your left hand at this point. And all your body weight is balanced on your right heel. That's the only part of you touching anything solid. And you're going 30 miles per hour with the doors wide open. It's shaking like an old man with ice in his drawers and even God is covering His eyes at this point. That sound safe to you?"

"No," Brian said.

"No, indeed. And if you should press too hard on the clutch and hit the brake instead, you're gonna stop real quick, but the hundred cases of milk in beautiful glass bottles don't have the sense to stop. They just keep going and you get splattered like a bug, but on the *inside* of the windshield instead of the outside."

"Oh," Brian said.

"You still want to know why we're in a Chevy?"

"Um, we're in a Chevy because we don't want to die in a Divco?"

"Very good, young fella," Ole Olson said. "Very good. See what a good teacher I am?"

"So welcome to Route 2. On our first stop, I'm going to show you how to carry bottles without using the carrier," Ole Olson said.

"Why?"

"Because it's something you need to know if you're going to be a good milkman. What if your carrier breaks? Or what if you lose it?"

"Okay," Brian said.

"When you're delivering up to five bottles, you don't need the carrier. I mean unless you're more comfortable using it. I'll show you how it works, and from there it will be up to you. Milkman's choice."

"Okay," Brian said.

"Alright then. This is the Flanagan house," Ole Olson said. "They get five quarts of whole milk," Ole Olson said. "Didn't I do a good job of picking the perfect customer for this lesson?"

Brian nodded and smiled.

"Come with me," Ole Olson said.

They got out of the truck and Ole Olson grunted up onto the sidestep. He reached into a case with the spread fingers of his left hand and grabbed the neck of two bottles, just below the paper caps. One was between his index and middle finger. The other was between his ring finger and his pinkie.

"You lift them like this, see?" Ole Olson whispered. He always whispered when he was outside near a customer's house.

Brian nodded.

"And then you lay a third bottle horizontally across your palm and hold it against the tops of the other two bottles with your thumb. Hop up here and try it."

Brian did.

"How's that feel?" Ole Olson said.

"Solid."

"You're carrying three quarts of milk in one hand. I can do that, too, but I wish my hands were as big as yours. You're a natural-born milkman, young fella. You'll have work forever. There will always be door-to-door milkmen. Nothing is *ever* gonna change that. You can take that to the bank."

Brian smiled.

"Now grab the other two bottles with your other hand, but first have your flashlight in that hand and hold it horizontal, like it's a third milk bottle"

"Got it?"

"Yes."

"Feel comfortable?"

"Yes."

"Okay, go."

Brian did as he was told. He was good that way.

Ole Olson backed into a street so the house was on Brian's side. Brian smiled, now used to this.

"Your turn again," Ole Olson said. "How about that! This here is the Weinreich house. They get six quarts of whole milk and a dozen eggs. Use the carrier."

"Where's the milk box?" Brian said.

"It's on the back stoop. It's dark back there so use your flashlight."

"Okay," Brian said and got out of the truck.

Ole Olson sat in the truck, smiling.

Waiting.

Ten-foot-tall Rose of Sharon bushes loomed along the whole length of the narrow driveway. Brian navigated around a Stingray bike left lying on its side, and a pair of roller skates, the kind that strap to your shoes and tighten with a skate key. He thought about stepping on one of those skates in the dark. He nudged them both to the side of the driveway with his new work shoes.

The backyard was overgrown with shrubs but he spotted the stoop right away and saw the milk box.

Then he heard the sound.

He shifted his light just in time to see the reflective eyes of a snarling German Shepherd charging at him from the other side of the yard. The dog didn't bark; it just snarled. Adrenaline hit Brian's body like electricity. He turned and started to run, but then he heard the dog gag and tumble against the collar as his chain pulled taut. The big dog was on his back, whimpering.

Brian turned his light on the animal, which was now up again on his hind legs and gagging and snarling against the collar. The dog had gone as far as he possibly could, which was about six feet away from the milk box. His eyes were murderous.

Brian waited another moment and then walked quickly to the milk box and made the delivery. The dog's teeth were bared and his eyes were bulging. Spittle dripped from his mouth, but he never barked.

Why?

Brian put the empties in the carrier and backed out of the yard. Once he cleared the dog's line of sight, he ran down the driveway, jumped onto the truck, slipped the empties into the crate, never taking his eyes off the driveway. And then he got into the truck and shut the door, being sure not to slam it.

"So," Ole Olson said. "What did you think of Klaus?"

"Klaus?" Brian said.

"The pooch in the backyard. The big German Shepherd. What did you think of him?"

"You *knew* he was back there?" Brian said.

"Of course, I've been delivering to Weinreich's since that pooch was a pup."

"Why didn't you warn me?" Brian said.

"Warn you? Why should I warn you? You go to horror movies, don't you?"

"Yes."

"Ever watch The Hound of the Baskervilles?"

"Sure. That one scared the heck out of me when I was a kid," Brian said.

"Well, you just met him again. His name is Klaus."

"He came *running* at me, Ole!" Brian said.

"I know. He runs at me, too, and that chain knocks him down every time. I'm still not used to it, but if I had warned you about him it would have taken all the fun out of it."

"Fun? You think that's fun?"

"Sure," Ole Olson laughed. "Horror movies are fun, aren't they?"

"Well, yeah, but still."

"So this is a horror movie come to life. It's also a lesson for you, young fella. You never know what's going to be in the next backyard. Always be ready for a surprise."

"Okay," Brian said.

"I told you I'm a good teacher, right?"

"Yes."

"Well, I'm *teaching* you. Always be ready for *anything* when you're alone in the night. *Anything* can happen."

"Okay," Brian said. His heartbeat was finally coming back to 50 beats a minute, his normal rate.

"Ole?"

"Yes?"

"Why doesn't Klaus bark?"

"He doesn't want to wake his owners. He respects their sleep. So do we."

"So that's why he doesn't bark?" Brian said.

"Well, yes. I asked him one night and that's what he told me. But, he also said that he hoped the chain would snap one of these nights before I could get back into the truck."

"Why?" Brian said.

"So he could eat me," Ole Olson said.

"What did you say to that?" Brian said.

"I told him to behave himself."

"What did he say?" Brian said.

"He just shrugged and said he was following his nature, just like everyone else in the world does, and that I should try to be more understanding of his needs."

"Oh," Brian said.

Ole Olson didn't ask Brian if he was worried about the draft because he knew Brian would probably get a deferment from the local draft board when he turned 18. Brian's only sibling, Sean, had died in Vietnam during the Tet Offensive the previous January. Sean had been just 19 years old. His father, Conor, had died a few weeks later, leaving no life insurance for Brian's mother, Grace.

Ole Olson never said that this was why he had given Brian the helper's job. He just told Grace McKenna that he sure could use a strong young fella like Brian to help him out during the summer, and on weekends and holidays after Brian went back to high school for his senior year.

"I'm not getting any younger," he told Grace McKenna and she agreed that her only remaining son would be a good helper for him. Silently, Grace McKenna thanked Saint Anthony, the patron saint of lost things, for answering her prayers. She could use the money Brian would contribute. It was just Brian and her now.

Ole Olson also told Grace that when Brian graduated from high school, he could work for him full time if he liked the work, and maybe even buy the route from him someday if things went well. Ole Olson promised to pay Brian a good salary.

Ole Olson hadn't charged Grace for a thing he delivered to their house ever since Conor died. He just couldn't. Nor would he talk to Brian about the now-dead Bobby Kennedy, who had tried to stop that war.

What was the point?

Ole Olson read the *Newsday*. He read it every day. He knew what was going on in the world, and most of it made no sense at all to him.

At Elizabeth, New Jersey's West Grand Station, two people in the enormous crowd that had gathered to watch Bobby Kennedy's funeral train pass by stumbled onto the adjacent tracks and died under the wheels of a second train, inbound from Chicago.

What was the *point* of that? Why had those people gone there to watch a train pass by? To stand on the tracks and risk their lives. To watch a *train*?

What was the point?

The whole world was going nuts. Martin Luther King was dead. Now Bobby Kennedy was also dead, as dead as his big brother, John. Riots were everywhere. American cities were on fire. And then there was this out-of-control war in Southeast Asia, with no end in sight.

Better to talk about good, clean milk in clear glass bottles.

Better to talk about dogs that lurk in backyards and never bark.

Better to talk about watching your back. Always.

Better to work in the night when most of the people in the world are asleep and unable to hurt you.

And better to talk about *silly* things, *impossible* things.

Like a roomful of *boobies*.

Much better.

Mommy

"Your school nurse left a message on the answering machine," Madeline Kepler said to her daughter, Hannah. "She said you were sick? What was that about? Are you sick?"

Madeline Kepler kept walking as she talked. She passed through the living room, where Hannah was on the couch, reading a book. She went into the bathroom. She didn't close the door.

Hannah didn't answer her.

"What was that *about*?" Madeline Kepler shouted from the bathroom.

Hannah kept reading her book.

"Hannah?" her mother shouted, now from the hallway. She was holding a mascara. "I'm *speaking* to you. Will you please *answer* me?"

"It was nothing," Hannah said without looking up from the book. "I sneezed on the bus. It happened so fast that I didn't have time to cover my mouth. People got upset. They made me sit in the nurse's office for a while to make sure I was okay. That's all."

"Will you please speak up? I can't *hear* you! Why do you mumble when I ask you a question? I can't stand the mumbling!"

"I said I *sneezed*," Hannah shouted, still without looking up.

"There's no reason for you to *shout!*" her mother shouted. "I'm not deaf!"

Hannah looked up, and then went back to her book.

"And for this they call me?" Madeline Kepler said, walking back into the bathroom. "For this? For *sneezing?*" she shouted. "Don't they have better things to do at that school of yours? Do they know I go to business? I should be concerned about a sneeze? It's not like you were bleeding. Were you bleeding?"

"No, I wasn't bleeding," Hannah said, loud enough to keep her mother from raising her voice even higher. "I just sneezed."

"Do I need to call her back?"

Hannah didn't answer.

Madeline Kepler walked back into the living room.

"I'm *asking* you. Do I need to call her *back*? She's probably not there now. It's late, and I don't have time to call her tomorrow. Does she know I go to business? I have no time for this." She walked back into the bathroom.

"I don't think she knows you go to business. She just knows that you're my mother."

"What? *Speak up!*"

Hannah said it again, louder.

"Well, I *do* go to business, and I don't have time for this nonsense. What's the *matter* with people these days that a sneeze should set off alarm bells? People sneeze. That's a normal thing to do. The sneezing. Who doesn't sneeze? Why are they calling *me?*"

Hannah said nothing.

Her mother was back.

"When does school end? I'm tired of this conversation."

"Friday," Hannah said.

66

"Good. I'm not calling her back. She shouldn't have called me in the first place."

Hannah said nothing.

"Have you decided what you're going to do this summer? Have you decided about camp?"

"I'm not going to camp," Hannah said.

"And why not? All the young people go to camp. I've told you that. It's how you meet someone nice, someone you might marry someday when you're grown up."

"I'm grown up now," Hannah said into her book.

"You're fourteen years old," her mother said. "You don't even have breasts yet. Fourteen and no breasts. And *pimples*. Does that sound grown up to you? *Oh, please!*"

"I'm not going to camp."

"Then what will you do with yourself all summer? I have to go to business. So does your father. And we'll be taking some weeks in France this summer. You know that. That's why we want you in camp. So we can go away with peace of mind. Your father needs a rest. So do I. You should go to camp."

"No, thank you."

"And we can't bring you to France, so don't even ask. Where we're staying is too nice. It's not for children. You wouldn't like it there. Your father needs to rest. So do I."

"I'll be fine here."

"So you say *now*. What will you be *then*? Please go to camp."

"No, mother. I have my books to read, a key to the house, and you'll leave me money. I know how to shop for food. I'll be fine. I'm not going to that camp. I can't stand those people."

"You don't even *know* those people," her mother said.

Hannah said nothing.

"How will you get to the food store if you stay here alone? You don't drive."

"I'll walk. It's a half-mile away. I know how to walk," Hannah said.

"How will you carry things?"

"With my arms."

"What if it rains?"

"I have an umbrella."

"I don't like this," her mother said. "But if that's what you want then *fine*; that's what you'll get. I'm sick to death of arguing with you. Don't blame me if something bad happens to you. Your father and I are not coming back if something bad happens to you. We need our rest. I'm warning you right now. We are *not* coming back!"

Hannah said nothing.

"This is ridiculous. I'm going to my nail appointment. I'll be back later. I'm not sure when. Did you wash your face? You should wash your face. Go wash your face. Did you ask the pretty girls about what brand of soap they use?"

Hannah said nothing.

"Did you, Hannah?"

Hannah said nothing.

Madeline Kepler picked up the keys to the Cadillac and slammed the front door.

Hannah went back to her book.

Bread
May 1969

Mr. Stein, the History teacher, was talking about the Cuban Missile Crisis and how close they all came to dying, even though they were too young to even know what was going on in 1962, and perhaps even now. He turned to the map on the wall to show them where the missiles had been.

"This crisis happened even though we have a military base there in Guantanamo." He leaned in and squinted at the map. "Ah, yes. It's right here," he said, touching a finger to the map.

Paul Thanatos used that moment to blow another spitball through his plastic straw. This one stuck in Hannah's hair. A titter went up in the class from those who saw what he had done. Paul Thanatos smiled, stuffed the straw under his right thigh, and looked up at the map as Mr. Stein turned around.

"Did I say something funny?" Mr. Stein said. Two girls giggled.

Hannah stood. She was six inches taller than Mr. Stein.

"Yes, Hannah? What is it? Do you need to be excused?"

"No, Mr. Stein. I just need to give Paul Thanatos a bigger target. He's shooting spitballs at me and I want to make sure he has fun."

"He's doing *what*?" Mr. Stein said.

"He's shooting spitballs at me." She reached into her hair and came out with the spitball. "Here's one," she said, holding it out on her open palm. "This is his latest. There are others on my back. I'm standing to give him a bigger target because doing this to me amuses him, and that's important."

The class exploded in laughter.

Hannah said nothing.

"Class! Please be quiet!" Mr. Stein said. "Paul, are you shooting spitballs at Hannah?"

"No," Paul Thanatos lied. He slumped down.

"Is someone else doing it?"

"No, It's just Paul Thanatos," Hannah said. "He does it often, and not just in your class. I don't mind him doing it because it amuses him. And that's important because he doesn't have much time left."

That stopped the laughter.

"Excuse me?" Mr. Stein said.

"He doesn't have much time left. Only a few more years. So he should enjoy himself."

"Bullshit," muttered Paul Thanatos.

"Paul, please watch your language in class," Mr. Stein said. "Hannah, what are you talking about?"

"Paul Thanatos, the boy with the spitballs. He's behind me," Hannah said, not turning to look. "He's going to die in a car accident on the Southern State Parkway when he's just eighteen years old. That's not long from now. Just a few years. Two of his friends will die with him: Jeffrey Bloom and Francis Dove. They have peaceful names, don't they? Bloom. Dove. They'll die anyway. Thanatos is a Greek name that is not as peaceful. It means death, but everyone dies, and when we die, our energy gets redistributed. Paul Thanatos' energy will go into a wheat field in central-North Dakota. It's very cold there in the winter. His energy will become bread that people will eat, and that's a wonderful thing, feeding people. But first Paul Thanatos and his two friends will die one hundred and twelve yards east of Exit Seventeen on the Southern State Parkway because their energy wants to get away from them. They'll die late at night. It will be in *Newsday*, but only for a day. Horrible accidents happen at that section of the parkway all the time."

"Bullshit!" Paul Thanatos spat, jumping out of his seat. "I'm not even taking Driver's Ed. I won't even have a car when I'm eighteen! My parents said I can't drive until I'm twenty-one. You're full of *shit*, Kepler!"

"Paul!" Mr. Stein said. "Your language. *Please*. Sit down!"

Paul Thanatos sat.

"You won't be driving," Hannah said, still not turning around. "You'll be one of the passengers. Jeffrey Bloom will be driving. Jeffrey Bloom really *likes* speed. You'll be very scared just before it happens, before you get to be bread. You'll wet yourself."

"Hannah!" Mr. Stein said.

"It's okay, Mr. Stein. That's why I don't mind his spitballs. It amuses him; and he doesn't have much time left. His energy will go on, though, and in a far better form than where it is now. He'll be bread."

"Bullshit!" Paul Thanatos screamed and contorted himself into a ball at his desk.

"Paul, please go to the Principal's office and wait there for me. Hannah, please stay after class."

The bell rang.

"Hannah, why did you *say* those things?"

"Which things, Mr. Stein?"

"About Paul dying and those two other boys dying with him. About Paul turning into bread. Why did you *say* that?"

"To scare him."

"To *scare* him?"

"Yes. And you never know," Hannah added. "It *could* happen that way. We'll just have to wait and see."

What's in my heart?
May 1969

Adele Bevin, or Mrs. B., as her students called her, sipped her tea and turned to the next essay. So far, the content of the essays had been pretty much what she had expected to hear from her ninth-grade students. The assignment had been to write 200 words on the theme: What's in my heart? The next essay was Jean Clark's, age 15.

What's in my heart?

What is in my heart is love for the Monkees. They are a band and they are on TV on The Monkees. The Monkees are four guys named, Mickey Dolenz, who used to be on TV in Circus Boy. That was on when I was a kid so I don't remember it but my mother remembers it. He is cute but not as cute as Davy Jones, who is a Monkee. Another Monkee is Michael Nesmith, who is funny and cute but not as funny and cute at Davy Jones. Another Monkee is Peter Tork, who is tall and cute, but not as cute as Davy Jones. I love Davy Jones. He is my favorite Monkee and he is always and forever in my heart. He sings a song called Daydream Believer. In this song he says this. Cheer up, Sleepy Jean. Oh, what can it mean? To be a Daydream Believer and a Homecoming Queen. He sings that to me. I am Sleepy Jean. I want to be a Daydream Believer and a Homecoming Queen and someday I want to marry Davy Jones even though he is short. I am also short and that's okay. He is in my heart.

Mrs. B. gave Jean Clark a B for decent spelling and grammar, and for making her point, as she saw it. She sipped her tea and reached for the next essay.

Whats in my hart?

The title of this esay is whats in my hart. I am Allan Pisani and I am in Mrs. Bevin's 9 grade english classe. I sit in the fort row. This esay is gonna be to hundred word long cause that is what Mrs. Bevin my english teacher said it should be. To hundred word. Thats a lot of word. It is. To hundred word.

I thout about this question alot and I think the answer is blud. That is what is in everybudys heart but onlee if they are alive. If they are dead the blud comes out because thats what they do at the funeral home. I no this because my grandpa dyed and I axed my father what happened to all the blud and he sez that the undertakor tuk it out with a thng that lukes like a gardin hose wit a sharp point but is different. I dont know exakly what it lukes like cause I never seen it up clos. I axed my father what they do wit the blud after they take it out and he sez they trow it down the toylet. I thought that was funny. The end of the esay.

Mrs. B. smiled and shook her head. It was exactly two-hundred words and she could see by the many small dots left by the tip of his pencil that Alan Pisani had counted the words several times, just to be sure. He was a delightful boy. Dumb as a rock, but sweet as can be.

She gave him a C for creativity, and wondered if she should have assigned a less poetic theme to children who are often quite literal.

Hannah Kepler's essay was next on her stack. She leaned back in her chair and noted again how small and neat Hannah's penmanship was. Hannah always strung her words tightly together, like small pearls on a necklace.
She read.

What's in my heart?
There is a blue eye in my heart that never blinks. It cannot. It must watch for and stop the small bullets they try to drill deeply into me, like the bullets that found the Kennedys.

Their bullets travel on the hard words that shoot from the rifle barrels of their cruel mouths. But I am taller than they are. My heart soars above them, and my blue eye sees beyond them to the sadness of their futures. My blue eye squints but never closes when they call me names. My heart embraces my blue eye, knowing that cruelty lurks everywhere, and that my blue eye must never blink. It will hold back the bullets trying to tear my heart apart. I know it will.

I am made of energy. I will die, but my energy will live on.

The rest of the 200 words you asked for wait in my heart, unspoken for now, but forever ready.

Mrs. B. let the paper drop to her lap. She stared at the wall. Shivered.

A half-hour later, after rereading it five times, Mrs. B. penned a red A+ at the top of Hannah's essay and added at the top of the page, Please see me.

The following day, Hannah didn't flinch when Mrs. B. laid the essay on her desk as she walked the classroom, returning the essays to her students. Mrs. B. looked down at her and paused. Hannah looked at the note on the paper and then up. She nodded.

"Your essay on what is in your heart is beautiful, Hannah," she said when they were together after class. "But it is also somewhat haunting."

"It is what is in my heart," Hannah said. "That was the assignment."

"I understand that, and you did a wonderful job with it," Mrs. B. said. "I gave you an A plus. You are my best student. But your words make me concerned for you, Hannah. Clearly, you're having problems with some people, and I care about you. Are you talking here about other students?" She pointed at the essay.

"Yes," Hannah said. "And other people that are not in this school as well."

"Are you thinking about hurting them, Hannah?"

"No."

"Are you thinking about hurting yourself?" Mrs. B. said.

"Not now. No. Why do you ask?"

"Because of this," Mrs. B. said, reading from the page. "I am made of energy. I will die, but my energy will live on."

"That's true," Hannah said.

"That you're made of energy, or that you will die?" Mrs. B. said.

"Both," Hannah said.

"I don't understand," Mrs. B. said. "Please help me to understand."

"We are *all* made of energy," Hannah said. "All of us. That's what life is. It's energy. It comes from the stars. From the universe. It was here before we were born and it will be here after we die. It gathered together to make us. We're made of the same stuff that everything else in the universe is made of. It's pure energy. It's neither good nor bad. It just *is*."

"But you also wrote that you will *die*," Mrs. B. said.

"Yes, we will *all* die, Mrs. B.," Hannah said. "You know that. Your husband died, didn't he?"

"Yes, he did, and I understand that, but are you thinking about hurting yourself, Hannah?"

"Not now. No," Hannah said.

"Do you want to talk to someone about this, Hannah? I can help you find someone to help you. A professional."

"I don't think so," Hannah said. "Not now. I'm fine now."

"Will you let me know if you change your mind? If you're *not* fine? If you start to have darker thoughts?"

"What are darker thoughts?" Hannah said.

"Thoughts of suicide," Mrs. B. said. "Thoughts of killing yourself?"

"Suicide isn't dark. *Nothing* is dark. Or *light*. It just is. I can't kill my energy," Hannah said. "I can cause it to move away from me if I choose to do that, and that would be *my* decision. But I can't possibly *kill* energy. It's eternal. When I die my energy will just leave this body and gather somewhere else, perhaps somewhere better than within this body."

"Where, for instance?" Mrs. B. said.

"Into a dog, or a cat, or some other animal, or a field of wheat, or a rock, or another human. Into anything. Energy is everywhere. Dying is just the movement of energy. It's nothing to fear. None of us actually goes away. We just reassemble as other things. We are made from stars."

"But these people that are trying to shoot bullets at you through their cruel words." She pointed at Hannah's essay. "What about *them*?"

"They're also energy. Everything is. I protect myself from them by being still. I'm not perfect at that yet. I do flare up now and then and strike back at them in my own ways, but I'm working on getting better. And quieter."

The late bell rang.

"I have to go now," Hannah said. "Is there anything else you'd like to know, Mrs. B.?"

"No, Hannah. I'm glad we spoke."

"I am, too, and I hope I helped you understand," Hannah said. "Thank you for caring about me."

She gathered her books and left for her next class. Didn't look back.

Mrs. B. stared at her hands in her lap.

Tuition

A car ran a red light and nearly hit the truck. Ole Olson swerved and hit the brakes. Stopped. Breathed deeply and stared at the car as it roared away.

"Gosh," Brian said. "That was close."

"It's easy to start thinking that we're out here all alone," Ole Olson said. "But we're working while the drunks are making their way home, so we always have to be on the lookout, especially after four o'clock. That's when the bars close for the night. It can get pretty crazy out here between four and four-thirty. After that, we're usually okay."

"You didn't honk your horn at that guy," Brian said. "Why?"

"I have *never* honked the horn on this truck, and neither will you," Ole Olson said, pointing at the center of the steering wheel. "Not once since I've owned it. I don't even know if it works. I have never honked a horn on *any* vehicle I have ever owned, no matter what happened."

"Why not?" Brian said.

"Because the truck has *brakes*. Why honk when I can brake? If I honk, I'm going to wake people up. They'll get out of bed, look out the window, see the name on the truck, not the idiot who cut us off, and then they'll tell everyone they know that Ole Olson woke them up in the middle of the night by honking his horn. That could kill this business. I know that for a fact, so I *never* honk, and you shouldn't either. Ever! If it wasn't illegal, I'd snip the wires to this horn." He pointed at it again. "Next to Fabrizio, a milk truck's horn is a milkman's worst enemy."

Brian nodded. It made sense.

"You should always listen to me, young fella. I have a lot to teach you. I do. *Listen*."

Brian nodded. Three times.

"Well, lookee here," Ole Olson chuckled. "We're at the Lindquist house and it just happens to be on *your* side of the truck." He tapped the route book. They get four beautiful quarts of whole milk. Go."

Brian hopped out of the truck, grabbed the four quarts of whole milk between his fingers and headed toward the back stoop. He was learning the route and Ole Olson no longer told him where the milk boxes were unless he asked, and Brian hardly ever did ask.

There was a heavy cobblestone on top of the Lindquist's milk box tonight. Brian looked at it, wondering. He set the milk bottles down on the stoop and moved the cobblestone next to the milk. Why was it there?

He was reaching for the box's lid when it banged open like a Jack in the Box and a black cat screeched and shot out. It clawed Brian's hand and disappeared into the dark bushes.

He stood still, waiting for his brain to catch up with his heartbeat. He looked at his scratched hand. It didn't hurt. He looked again.

Okay.

That was a *cat*, right?

A cat.

Right?

"What took you so long back there? Ole Olson said when Brian slid back into the truck.

"There was a cat in the milk box. A cobblestone was holding the lid closed."

"Ah, the old cat-in-the-milk-box trick!" Ole Olson laughed. "Well, I have to say you're certainly getting your baptism by fire, young fella."

"You've had that happen to you?"

"More times than I can count. The only thing worse than a cat in the milk box is a toad in the milk box. They jump when you put the milk in the box. In the dark, toads are the creepiest things there are. They are one of the reasons why I have gray hair."

"Who *does* these things?" Brian said.

"Kids. They think giving the milkman a heart attack is funny."

"I don't think it's funny."

"Well, you'll get used to it," Ole Olson chuckled. The next time you see a stone on top of a milk box you'll open that box *very* carefully. And do you know what we call all of this stuff, young fella?"

"What?"

"Milkman's tuition," Ole Olson said and laughed. They don't teach this stuff in that school of yours. The only way to learn it is to get out here and do it. That's Milkman's tuition. And watch out for those warty toads. They don't come with cobblestones."

Sean

"Are you sure?" Brian asked his brother.

"I'm not college material, Bri. I didn't like high school and if I don't sign up they're going to draft me anyway. At least this way I get to choose my service, and maybe even what I want to do once I'm in."

"What will you choose?" Brian said.

"I think I have to try out for the Marines," Sean said.

"Why?"

"Because Dad was a Marine. You know all his stories as well as I do. He never misses a chance to tell them. All he talks about is war and how much fun he had killing the enemy."

"So you have to be a Marine because he was a Marine?"

"I think he'd be angry if I wasn't. He'd probably call me a draft dodger if I wasn't in the Marines."

"But how could he do that if you were in one of the other services?" Brian said.

"You know how he gets," Sean said. "It's Marines or else."

Brian said nothing.

"He'll feel the same way about your choice if this war goes on. Are you thinking about college? That can get you a deferment for a while."

"What's that?" Brian said.

"A deferment? It means you get to go to school and grow up some more before you have to go fight in the war."

"I don't know anything about college. I don't even know where college is."

Sean tousled his kid brother's hair. "It's not in one particular *place*," he said. "College is all over Long Island. There's one in Farmingdale. That's real close. There's another one in Hempstead. There are a few more on the North Shore and the South Shore. You could try to get into one of them. It would be good for you to learn more things. That's what you do in college. You learn more things."

"Does college cost money?" Brian said. "I don't have much money, and I'm saving for a car."

"It costs something but I don't know how much. You could get a better job than delivering the *Newsday*. Walk over to the factories on Division Avenue before school is out and ask for a summer job. They hire strong young guys like you."

"Doing what?" Brian said.

"I don't know. Mostly working in the warehouse, I guess. It's hard work but you're up for it. You could probably make enough money to get into one of the colleges when you're done with high school and still have enough money to get your car. That would keep you out of the war."

Brian said nothing.

"I'm going to sign up with the Marines tomorrow," Sean said. "I'll take the bus over to Hempstead. That's where the recruiting office is."

"Does Dad know?"

"No, I haven't told him," Sean said. "I'll let it be a surprise. Brian said nothing.

The Landing Strip
October 1968

Richie plucked Brian's shortie off the bar and filled it with ice-cold Schaefer beer, leaving a nice head on top.

"Sorry, Brian," Richie said, holding the glass up to the light. "I always try to put the head on the bottom, but it just keeps floating up to the top. Why it does that is anyone's guess."

Brian smiled but said nothing. Richie hadn't asked if Brian wanted another. He just knew. He set the glass on the cardboard coaster in front of Brian and rapped the bar twice with his knuckles.

"On me," he said.

Brian smiled and nodded, but said nothing.

"You want a shot?"

"No thanks," Brian said. "I'm good with just the beer."

Richie leaned in and whispered, "You're a smart fella." He nodded and winked.

Brian said nothing.

The Landing Strip was Brian's college. He was learning a lot during the hour he spent there just about every afternoon. He'd put a dollar on the bar and have four short beers, which cost him sixty cents because one of the beers was always free. He always left the change for Richie. Sean had told him to do that.

Brian loved listening to the older men talk about the airplane factories, and their bosses, and what was going on that weekend with their wives and their kids. They also talked about their wars and what they did in Europe, and the Pacific, and in Korea. They'd argue about which was the toughest place to be, but never too much. All of it had been tough. They all knew that.

The older men talked about President Truman and how they might not be sitting on those stools right now, had that man not dropped those atomic bombs on Japan.

"I hope that great man lives forever," Jake said. "He did the right thing with those bombs."

There were nods all around.

The airplane men reminded Brian of his brother, Sean, and that's why he started coming in here. He was trying to make sense of it all.

But some of these men had mixed feelings about Vietnam.

"I guess the war is good for the airplane business. We get plenty of overtime," Andy said, "But I think we're losing too many good men in this one. And they're all dying for nothing. This war is senseless, not like *our* war. Our war was a good war. It made sense. This one doesn't."

Brian thought of Sean, in his grave in the Pinelawn Cemetery just three miles from his barstool. He sipped his beer.

Richie leaned in on Andy and whispered something.

"Hey, Brian, no offense meant by what I just said about the war," Andy said. "I'm sorry about your brother. He was a great guy, and very generous when his ship came in."

Brian nodded, but said nothing.

Since Sean's death, Brian had settled into a rhythm of listening to people, and speaking only when asked a question. The only exception to this was when he was with Ole Olson. He would always ask Ole Olson questions. He was trying to understand why that was. Perhaps it was because Ole Olson rarely asked *him* questions. Ole Olson preferred to talk, and he talked nearly nonstop.

"You finished with school for good now, Brian?" Andy said, trying to get past the awkwardness of his comment about the war.

"I am."

"Are you going to do the milk full-time now?"

"Yes. I'm Ole Olson's helper. I'll help him every night. To make money. For my mother."

"I know you like doing the milk, Brian. Richie tells me you're real good at it," Andy said.

Brian said nothing.

"You do like it, don't you?" Andy said.

"Yes, very much," Brian said.

"What do you like most about it?" Andy said.

"I like looking at the water towers when it's dark outside and the red lights up on top of them are going on and off. The towers look like huge aliens."

"I never thought about them that way," Andy said. "But I can see what you mean. What else do you like about your job?"

"I like working with Ole Olson. He's a good guy."

"I hope you don't ever have to go to war," Andy said. "I'm hoping the draft board gives you the exemption. Your mother needs you."

Brian looked at him but said nothing. Andy hadn't asked a question.

"You don't want to go to war, do you, Brian?"

"No," Brian said. "I want to do the milk."

"I didn't want to go to war either," Andy said. "But that's what I had to do. I had no choice. I wish I could have done the milk instead. It was pretty horrible, my war."

87

Brian said nothing.

"Hey, Richie, give Brian a beer on me, willya?" Andy said.

Richie smiled and set an upside-down shot glass in front of Brian's beer.

Brian smiled at Andy but said nothing.

Andy sipped his beer and went quiet.

Jake stared at Brian.

Shook his head.

Sipped his beer.

Grace

"You killed him, Conor," Grace McKenna said to her husband. "You with all your proud war talk for all these years. You with all your glory. You with your guns and your bullets and your war souvenirs hidden in cabinets and closets all over my house. *You.* You sent him there to die."

"How could you say such a thing to me? I'm your *husband*." Conor hissed. "Our son is *dead*. He is in God's good hands now."

"You killed him," Grace said.

"The *Viet Cong* killed him, not I," Conor said. "*Not I.* He did his duty for his country. He died like a man in the line of duty. He was a hero. I am not guilty of this. I did not kill my *son*." He smacked the end table so hard it jumped. His face strained pinker.

"He wouldn't have gone there if not for you and all your fine talk of guns and killing, and how much *fun* you had during your stinking war," Grace said. "How many people you killed."

"Those were not people," Conor McKenna shouted. "Those were the *enemy!* It was kill or be killed."

"But you loved it so. You did. And I'll not forgive you, Conor McKenna. Not ever. You murdered our boy. Our *son*. And you'll not murder our other son. I'll see to that. He's all I have now."

She got up and left the room.

When they spoke again some days later, it was with clipped words that carried no love. Tea? No. Is it too cold? I'm fine. What would you like for dinner? I don't care.

She sat in the widow's chair at Conor McKenna's wake and started at the closed casket, red rosary beads dripping off her clenched fists. She did not cry. Nor did she ask her remaining son any questions.
So Brian said nothing.

Watermelon Sugar

"In watermelon sugar the deeds were done and done again as my life is done in watermelon sugar."

Hannah read the opening sentence of Richard Brautigan's new novel, *In Watermelon Sugar,* three more times, falling into its cadence and poetry and wanting to sit with this older man who had written this book, and ask him questions about the magical world that he had created, a world filled with death delivered to close relatives by tigers that talk, gentle sex, and suicide.

Who *was* this man?

Where was this place called iDEATH, where everything was made of watermelon sugar?

She had so many questions.

She lay awake, listening in the chirping night for the milkman's truck and the white tinkling of his bottles. He would be here soon. He always was. The milk was cool and sweet in the mornings. It was honest and she loved it.

Her mother had called from Paris and then again from Provence. She and her father had been gone for two weeks and would be back soon, or so her mother had said. Soon. There was no definite date. "Behave yourself. Your father needs his rest.

You should have gone to camp," she told Hannah during their first, very brief ("These calls are so *expensive!*") phone call. Her father had not gotten on the phone, which was fine with Hannah.

As he had with the dogs and the cats and the toads, Brian had grown used to the people who did not sleep, and who would ask for something they wanted in the night. Most were older woman with curlers in their hair, cold cream on their faces, and cigarettes in their mouths. They would open the door quickly, but only by a few inches, and they would say, "Milkman, milkman?" And Brian, startled, would look up from the open maw of their milk box and chirp, "Yes?" and the woman would ask for a half-pint of heavy cream, or one of the other miscellaneous items that was not on their order, and Brian would say, "Yes," and run back to the truck to ask Ole Olson if it was okay. Ole Olson would say sure and write a note, and place it on the customer's page in the route book.

When Brian returned to the stoop with the item, the door would always be closed and the older woman would be gone. He'd leave what she wanted in the milk box and rush back to the truck.

One time, an older man lingered at the door and asked Brian if he was lonely.

"No, Ole Olson is in the truck," Brian said.

"Would you like to visit with me for a while?" the older man said.

"No, thank you. We have to move on. Ole Olson is waiting for me, and the ice is melting," Brian said.

"Perhaps when you finish you could come back and visit with me. I can make you breakfast. You are very beautiful," the older man said.

"No, thank you. We have to return the truck to the dairy so they can wash the milk bottles and fill them again. And then I have to take a shower and help my mother."

The older man nodded sadly and whispered the door closed.

Brian said nothing of this to Ole Olson.

Hannah's parents didn't have air-conditioning in 1968. She lay awake with her screened windows open and listened to the persistent whir of the small, oscillating fan as it moved moist air back and forth across her long, slender body.

She thought of watermelon sugar.

Christmas 1968

Brian, who had not gone back to school for his senior year, kissed his mother at 6 PM on December 24, 1968 and went to bed.

As he slept, Frank Borman, Jim Lovell, and Bill Anders spun silently around the Moon. Light into darkness. Light into darkness. Light into darkness.

Ten times.

A photo of Earth, mailed from the Moon, showed a fragile blue globe stuck on the vast, velvet blackness of space. Seeing this lonely photo, millions of people wondered how there could possibly be a thing called war.

The astronauts read aloud the first 10 verses of Genesis, and then the world heard Commander Frank Borman's staticky voice say, "From the crew of Apollo 8, we close with good night, good luck, a Merry Christmas – and God bless all of you, all of you on the good Earth."

Brian slept through it all.

He dreamt of hail hitting the window. It wouldn't stop.
Tap, tap.
Tap, tap, tap.
Persistent, like a heartbeat.
He woke and looked at the clock he had forgotten to set.

Tap, tap.

He sprang up and raised the shade. Ole Olson was tapping the screen on his window with the handle of the broken-glass broom he kept behind the seat. He did not look happy. He pointed at his wristwatch and waddled back to the truck. Brian joined him in less than five minutes.

"Sorry," he mumbled.

"Forget to set the clock?"

"It didn't go off. I must have forgotten. Sorry," Brian said.

"Well, you'll just have to move faster tonight," Ole Olson said. "And we're lucky that it's Christmas. People sleep in on Christmas. Merry Christmas, by the way!" He reached over and shook Brian's hand.

"I'm really sorry, Ole. I don't know how I let that happen."

"Ah, we all make mistakes, young fella. That's how we learn. Milkman's tuition. I'll let it go this time, but if it happens again, you'll be dining on my specialty of the day." He held up his fist.

"Knuckle sandwich?" Brian said.

"Yep," Ole Olson said and punched him lightly on his thigh. "The 'ol knuckle sandwich."

It was 19 degrees and the thin gloves Brian wore weren't doing much good. But thicker gloves didn't work on the route because he needed to feel the milk bottles between his fingers. He drew four bottles from the top case, missing the sad sound of falling ice chips, which certainly weren't needed on this night. He headed for the milk box on the back stoop. Fortunately, this wasn't a white Christmas.

After a hurried stop at the diner that morning, Ole Olson had told him about the time he had slipped and fallen into a snowdrift in one of the darker backyards during a white-Christmas blizzard.

"I had eight bottles of milk in the carrier. When I went down, all the bottles buried themselves in the snow." Ole Olson laughed at the memory as they drove. Brian smiled at the windshield.

"I didn't have my flashlight because I was in a hurry to finish. It was so miserable that night. It took me a while to find all the milk bottles in the snow. White snow, white milk, clear glass, he belched. "Pardon me, I meant to throw up," he chuckled.

"I'm glad that hasn't happened to me," Brian said.

"The belching?"

"No, losing the milk in the snow."

"Well, it hasn't happened to you *yet*, young fella. It's gonna happen to you sooner or later if you stick with me. All of it. That's the life of a milkman. It may seem monotonous at times, all this driving and delivering, but there's a surprise waiting around every turn. That's the god's truth." He belched again.

"Did you mean to throw up, Ole?" Brian smiled.

"Yep!" Ole Olson said, and belched again. "It's the fried onions. Want me to bring it up again so we can vote on it?"

Brian smiled at the windshield.

The insides of the thin gloves, scratched the warts on his hands. He would put some of his mother's cold cream on them when he got home, but for now, he would just have to put up with it.

Last September, when Brian first noticed the warts, he asked Ole Olson about them. Ole Olson told him that the water from the ice causes the warts and Brian believed him. Neither man knew that human papillomavirus is the true cause or warts, and that you get it by touching people who have the HPV.

"Warts are an occupational hazard, young fella," Ole Olson had said. "Our hands are soaking wet for a good part of the year and the water makes warts grow, just like it makes the flowers grow. Yep, it's the water and the toads in the milk boxes that get them going. The toads touch the boxes; we touch the boxes. Our hands are wet, and the next thing you know, we got the warts, just like the toads do. Take my word for it. It's the god's truth and there's nothing we can do about it. It's just part of the job."

Ole Olson reached over to shake Brian's hand, which he often did when he was making a point and he needed Brian to agree with him.

And *that's* how Brian got the HPV.

Ole Olson pulled up to the Kepler house and glanced at the route book. "Just two quarts today," he said. "Mrs. Kepler said she and her husband were going skiing and that their daughter was the only one home. I don't think it's right to leave a young girl home by herself, especially on Christmas, but the Keplers are Jewish, and Hanukkah is over, so who am I to judge? Go bring the young lady her two quarts of fresh milk."

"Okay," Brian said, opening the door.

He hurried to the back stoop and opened the milk box. He shone his light into the box to see if there were empty bottles, or an envelope with money in there. There was neither, but there was a note, written in pencil on pink paper. The lettering was small, tight, and neat.

Do you have watermelon sugar today?

Confused, Brian carried the note back to the truck and showed it to Ole Olson.

"What the heck is watermelon sugar?" Ole Olson said.

"I don't know. I thought you would know," Brian said. "You know about everything."

"Well, I don't know about this. I mean watermelons are sweet, sure, but what does that have to do with what *we* do? It must be a note from the kid. Kids do some crazy things. As we *both* know," Ole Olson smiled at Brian.

"What should we do?" Brian said.

Ole Olson took a pencil and wrote on the bottom of the paper: Sorry. We don't have watermelon sugar today. Maybe Santa will bring it for you.

"Here, take it back and put it in the box."

Brian read it, smiled, and then did as he was told. He was good that way.

"Do you believe in Santa?" Brian said.

"Sure! I see him out working every Christmas. We're the only ones out working on Christmas morning. It's just me, you, and Santa and his reindeer. Sometimes he slides down the roof when I'm putting the milk in the boxes. That only happens when it's snowing, though. Most of the time he just winks at me and then I wink back. We're just a couple of old fat guys trying to get the work done. Let's keep an eye out for him tonight." Ole Olson chuckled.

"Okay," Brian said.

"I like Christmas because the customers sleep in. I mean except for the Jews. They get up and go to work. They have Hanukkah, not Christmas."

"Do Jews believe in Santa Claus?" Brian said.

"Depends on the Jew," Ole Olson said.

Brian thought about that for a while.

"What about Jesus?" Brian said.

"What about him?" Ole Olson said.

"He was Jewish, right?"

"Yes."

"But he believed in Christmas, right?"

"Well, Christmas was his birthday, so I suppose he believed in it," Ole Olson said. "Do you believe in *your* birthday?"

"What do you mean?"

"What do you mean what do I mean?" Ole Olson said. "Do you believe you were born?"

"Sure. I'm here. I must have been born," Brian said.

"Well, there you go then. Only people who were born can believe they were born, and since Jesus was born on Christmas he must believe in Christmas. They even named the day after him, which is more that they did for you or me. Make sense?"

"I guess so," Brian said.

"Good. What else is on your mind, young fella? I got all the answers," he chuckled.

"Was there Santa Claus then, Ole?" Brian said.

"In Jesus' time? I don't think so. I think he came later."

"Who made him up?" Brian said.

"Santa Claus?"

"Yes," Brian said. "Who made him up?"

"Who says Santa Claus is made up?" Ole Olson said, smiling in the dark. "Didn't I just tell you I see him every year when I'm doing the milk? Keep your eyes peeled, young fella. He could show up at anytime."

Brian said nothing, but he did smile.

With less than an hour to go on the route, Ole Olson belched again but this time he grabbed the right side of his belly and groaned.

"What's wrong?" Brian said.

"I don't know," Ole Olson said. "Just got a stabbing pain. Feels like somebody put a steak knife in me. Let me pull over here for a second."

He pulled to the curb, set the brake, and grimaced.

"You okay?" Brian said.

"I don't know. It hurts like hell. Let me get out or the truck and walk around a bit. It must be the onions. It feels like gas, but worse," he gasped. *"Much worse."*

He slid from the truck and immediately doubled over in pain. He threw up in the street. Brian leaped out of the truck, ran around and put his hands on Ole Olson's arms. He guided him to the passenger side of the truck.

"What are you doing?" Ole Olson gasped.

"I'm going to take you to the hospital," Brian said. "You may be having a heart attack."

"No, I'll be okay. Just let me rest a bit. We gotta do the milk. I gotta clean up this mess I just made. Can't stop. People depend on us" He bent over again and cried out in pain.

"I'm *taking* you," Brian said, moving the heavy man toward the truck.

"Okay," Ole Olson said. "Okay."

Brian drove to Plainview Hospital, which was less than a mile away. He helped Ole Olson out of the truck. It was five-thirty in the morning and there were just a few people sitting around a sad, silver Christmas tree in the waiting room.

"I think he's having a heart attack," Brian said to the nurse at the desk. She called for help and a team came quickly.

"Call my wife," Ole Olson gasped as they were wheeling him away. "And watch the milk."

Brian called Ole Olson's wife, Mae, from the nurse's station and she said she would be right there. He told her that he was going to finish the route. She was too upset to say that he shouldn't do that.

Brian found his way back to the last house they had delivered to and followed the codes in the route book to the finish. He knew the route fairly well, but just to be sure, he used the book. When he was done, he went back to the hospital.

"He's in surgery," Mae said.

"What's wrong with him?"

"It's his gallbladder. The doctor is removing it now."

"Is that in his belly? He had a real bad bellyache. Is it serious?" Brian said.

"Yes, it's in his belly, but he's in very good hands now. Thank you for bringing him here."

"What should I do now?" Brian said.

"Well, you can wait here if you'd like, but he'll be in surgery for a while, and then he'll be in recovery."

"I want to take the truck back to the dairy," Brian said. "So they can wash the bottles and fill them up again with milk. I'll come back later to see how he is, if that's okay with you."

"That's fine with me. You did the right thing by bringing him here, Brian. Thank you, and Merry Christmas," she said.

"Merry Christmas," Brian mumbled and left.

"What's wrong?" Grace McKenna said when he walked in.

"Ole is real sick. I had to take him to the hospital. They said it was his gallbladder. That's in his belly. They're operating on him now."

"Sweet Jesus," his mother said, blessing herself. "I hope he's alright. We need this job. I mean *you* do."

"I know, ma," Brian said. "*We* do. I finished the route all by myself. After I brought him to the hospital, I finished it. The whole rest of the route. All by myself."

"Ah, my boy," Grace McKenna said, hugging him. "I'm so proud of you. Merry Christmas, my good boy. Merry *Christmas.*"

"Merry Christmas," Brian mumbled. His head twitched three times.

Brian showered, ate, and went back to the hospital early that afternoon. Mae was in the semi-private room with Ole Olson.

"Well, young fella," Ole whispered. "You did me a good turn. And you delivered the milk."

"I did," Brian said. "And I brought the empties back to the dairy to get them washed and filled for tonight."

"Brian did all that for us," Mae said, holding Ole Olson's hand. "He's a good boy."

"He's a good *man*," Ole Olson said.

"I didn't want to get a knuckle sandwich," Brian said and smiled.

"Don't make me laugh, Brian. It hurts." Ole Olson laughed anyway.

"So what did they do to you?" Brian said.

"They took out my gallbladder," Ole Olson said. "I don't need it anyway, and I'm much better now."

"But he's going to be out of work for a while, Brian," Mae said. "It could be weeks, maybe longer. I don't know what we're going to do."

"I can do the routes for you," Brian said. "I *know* I can. Let me do them. Please."

Ole Olson and Mae looked at each other.

"Do you think you're ready for that?" Mae said.

"I think he is," Ole Olson said.

"Thank you," Brian said. "I'll make sure I don't make any mistakes."

"You'd better not, or else," Ole Olson said, smiling and lifting his fist a few inches off the bed.

Brian smiled, but said nothing.

"And when you do the milk without me, you're getting twenty-five bucks a night instead of fifteen, young fella," Ole Olson said. "I don't want to hear any argument about that."

Brian smiled. "Gee, thanks, Ole. *Thanks.*"

Brian would be making more money in a week than his dead father had ever made in a week, but that never occurred to him at the time.

"Why did you say you were going to pay him that much?" Mae said after Brian had left. "Are you out of your mind?"

"He's worth every penny of it, Mae." Ole Olson said. "And we need him right now."

"You should have offered him twenty, not twenty-five. I *need* that money."

"Brian needs it, too, Mae. He's supporting his mother."

"Well, you're supposed to be supporting *me*," Mae said, "but now it looks like you're more concerned for that kid than you are for your own wife. We need that *money*."

"We'll still be making plenty of money even after we pay him," Ole Olson whispered. "You know that. You keep the books. You know how much we make. We can easily afford Brian making twenty-five a night."

"That's not the *point*. You didn't have to promise him so much. He would have kept doing the route for fifteen bucks a night. He thinks it's fun. It's a game for him. He's just a dumb kid."

"No, he's not dumb, Mae. He's a good young man who probably just saved my life. And he finished the route all by himself to boot. He's capable. He's money in the bank for us. He can keep us in business until I can get back on my feet. He saved my life, Mae."

"No, the *surgeon* saved your life," Mae spat. "Not that kid."

"Ah, c'mon, Mae. Have a heart," Ole Olson said.

Mae shook her head in disgust and left the room.

Delaney's 2018

He turned his attention from the street and the Mustang that was no longer there.

"You okay?" Apple said.

He smiled. "Yeah, I'm okay. Just wandering down Memory Lane."

"For awhile there, I thought you were going to need a passport to get back to me," Apple said.

He laughed.

"What's your name?" Apple said.

"Brian," he said. "Brian McKenna."

"Pleased to meet you, Brian McKenna," Apple said, reaching over the bar. "You tell a good story."

Brian took her hand and shook it. Strong

"I have enough stories to last me a lifetime," he said.

"Tell me another one," Apple said. "Make it a happy one."

Brian smiled and looked down into his beer.

"When I was eighteen," he said. "I was running the milk route all by myself. I had dropped out of school and I did the milk full-time. I think it was the best job I ever had." He looked up.

"Why did you leave school?" Apple said.

"Because I hated school, and my mother was a widow and we needed the money." Brian said.

"Ah, the good son," Apple said. "Any siblings?"

"I had a brother. Sean. He died in Vietnam. He was just nineteen years old. He'll always be my big brother, no matter how old I get." He raised his pint and toasted the empty space between them. Sipped.

"I'm sorry," Apple said.

"Me, too. We were close. He volunteered for the Marines," Brian said. "He died on the first day of the Tet Offensive. January 30, 1968. I was seventeen years old that year."

"So sad," Apple said.

"He used to come in here for a beer, too. Before me."

"Really? This place is starting to sound like a family affair." She laughed.

"Richie used to run a race book in here. It was illegal but no one cared. The airplane guys and everyone else would place their bets with him."

"He did this on his own?" Apple said.

"I used to wonder about that, but I don't see how he could have. There was a *lot* of money involved. I never played. I couldn't afford to. There must have been others involved. People Richie knew."

"So where's the happy part of this story?" Apple said.

"Sean hit it big on the Superfecta one week. You have to pick the first four horses to finish, and in the exact order. First, second, third, and fourth. It's really hard to do that."

"I can imagine," Apple said.

"He won six-thousand bucks in here. He was just eighteen years old when that happened. The same age as me the first time I walked in here to drink with the men."

"Wow. Six-thousand! That must have been a fortune back then," Apple said.

"It was about a year's salary," Brian said, hoisting his pint and smiling. "And beers were just twenty cents."

"So what did he do with the money?"

"He put a hundred bucks on the bar and bought drinks for all the guys until it was gone, and then he put the rest of it in the bank. For his *future*."

Brian sipped his beer.

"Oh, my god. He never got to spend it?"

"Nope."

"So what happened to it?"

"He had a bankbook. He told me about it but he never told me where he kept it. He thought he was going to die an old man. I figured he hid it somewhere in the house. I didn't think he told my parents that he won the money because they would have been upset that he was gambling. He was a good son too."

"So?" Apple leaned in. "What happened?"

"I looked just about everywhere for it but couldn't find it. My mother passed on a few years later and she left the house to me, I was going through some letters that Sean had sent her from Vietnam. In one, he told her about the bankbook and where he had hidden it. He told her not to tell our father."

"Why?"

"I don't know," Brian said

"So where was it?" Apple said.

"He hid it in the basement. It was up in the ceiling by the boiler. My mother had never touched it. I guess she figured it was his business and not hers. And then when he died she was grief-stricken. She never mentioned it to me."

"Were you able to get the money?"

"Yes, and the interest it had earned as well."

"What did you do with it?"

"I invested it in some things and it grew a lot. Then, after a few years, I sold the house. Houses around here had gone up a lot in value by the Eighties."

"I know. So where did you go?" Apple said.

"I bought a small camper and traveled the country. I spent years just bouncing around, working odd jobs. Just moving from here to there. I even tended bar for a while."

"Gosh, what a life you've had."

Brian smiled.

"Are you married?" Apple said.

"No, I never was."

"Why not?"

"I don't know. It just never happened."

"I get that," Apple said.

Brian said nothing.

"How did your mother die?" Apple said, changing the subject.

"Cancer. She loved her Newports. They say those menthol cigarettes will kill you, and they sure did kill her."

"When did your father pass away?"

"A couple of weeks after Sean did."

"Oh my god! How did he die?"

"He went out to our garage one afternoon when my mother was watching her soap opera on the TV. *Search for Tomorrow* was its name, and that proved appropriate. My father shot himself in the head with a forty-five automatic he had brought home from his war in the Pacific," Brian said.

"And this is the *happy* story?" Apple said, raising her eyebrows.

"Happy stories often have sad parts," Brian said.

"Why did he do it? Your father."

"No one knows. He didn't leave a note. He just went out to the garage like he was taking out the garbage. Never came back. I have no idea why he did it. My mother never talked about him again. Not once. And she never cried at his wake or at his funeral. I don't know why."

"Did you ask her?"

"No. I just couldn't. All I could do was be there for her. And I was, right up to the end."

"I am so sorry."

"It was a lifetime ago," Brian shrugged. "Life goes on."

"It does," Apple said.

"Oh bla dee, oh blah dah," Brian said, raising his glass.

Apple raised her coffee mug.

The man down the bar raised his hand.

Apple looked at him.

"Another?" she said.

"Please," he said.

Brian gestured toward the empty stool.

"Like to join us?" he said down the bar.

The man shook his head. Didn't smile.

"No," he said. "I'm good."

"Shh. Don't," Apple whispered. "Let him stay right where he is. Believe me, it's for the best."

She went to get the man his longneck Bud.

Iced Milk
July 1969

The July air from the fan moved across Hannah's long body. She thought of the coolness of the milk bottles, wet from the ice, but still out there on the milk truck. She would love to lie down on that ice. Now. To stretch across it all. To melt into it. Now.

It was so hot now.

The milk would be here soon.

Brian moved like a piston between the truck and the milk boxes, trying to get back to Long John Nebel on the AM radio as quickly as possible. The talk tonight was about UFOs. Brian glanced out the truck's open window and upward before letting out the clutch. The houses in this neighborhood were new and the trees the builder had planted were still short. The sky went on forever here. If the aliens were really up there in their UFOs, he'd be the one to see them. He was the only person awake in the whole world just then. Ole Olson had told him that so many times, and he wanted to see a UFO tonight, or watch a water tower tear its spidery feet from the earth and stomp around, free at last. He wanted to see something important. Anything important. He wanted to believe in something. *Anything.*

Hannah checked the clock on her nightstand. It was 3:25 AM. She threw her long, slender legs over the side of her bed and stood. Her hair was pillow-wild. She didn't care. She walked to the kitchen, moved a wooden chair close to the back door where the milk box was. Sat in the dark.

Waited.

Crickets scratched at the dark.

Brian, flashlight in hand, flipped the lid of the milk box open with his right pinkie. There were four empties in the box. No note. No money. He lifted the empties, two at a time, and set them on the stoop. He placed four quarts of cold, whole milk in the box and closed the lid.

"Do you have watermelon sugar tonight?" A whisper.

Brian looked up. Looked around. No one.

"Do you?" Quieter still. A soft breeze.

"I don't," he said to the air. "No. I don't." His head turreted around.

"Why not?"

"I don't know what it is," Brian said. "What is watermelon sugar?"

"It is all that is *sweet*. All that is good."

"Who *are* you?" Brian said.

"My name?"

"Yes."

"I'm Hannah. But you can call me Margaret if you'd like. That's the name of the girl in the story."

"What story?" Brian said.

"*In Watermelon Sugar*," Hanna whispered. "Margaret tied the end of her scarf to a branch covered with young apples. And then she stepped off the branch and stood by herself in the air. Isn't that so beautiful?"

"Why did she do that?" Brian whispered to the dark.

"To set her energy free," Hannah said. "Her energy didn't want to be in her body anymore. She listened to it, and set it free."

"I think I'll call you Hannah instead of Margaret," Brian whispered. "Hannah is a nice name."

"Okay. That's fine."

"Where are you?" Brian whispered.

"Here. In the kitchen."

"Hannah, we don't deliver watermelon sugar. I'm sorry."

"But you deliver cool milk that is beautiful," she said. "Icy cool and beautiful." Her voice lilted off and away, like white smoke in the darkness.

"Yes."

"Milk is like watermelon sugar," Hannah said.

"Is it?"

"It is."

Quiet.

"May I see your truck?" Hannah said.

"What?"

"Your truck. May I come outside and see your truck? You're truck carries the cool ice and the beautiful milk. May I touch the ice and the milk bottles? It's very hot tonight. I'd like to touch the ice and the bottles. I need to feel the mothers."

"The mothers?" Brian said.

"Yes."

"Um, okay." Brian said. "I guess that's okay. Sure. Why not?"

The door opened.

The Landing Strip
July 20, 1969

Andy raised his beer and tapped the bar with his knuckles.

"Guys, glasses up to our brave men who are now walking on the Moon. We did it!"

They all toasted and drank.

"They're up there right now with my Lem," Andy said.

"Jeez, Andy. *Your* Lem," Pete said. "You build it all by yourself?"

"No," Andy said. "I had some help, but it still feels like it's mine. How many men in the history of the world can say they were a part of building the Lunar Module?"

"From the size of Grumman, I'd say tens of thousands," Pete laughed.

"Ah, you Republic guys are just jealous," Andy said.

"I wish we were *still* Republic guys," Pete said.

"Me, too," Andy said. "I don't like what Fairchild is doing to you guys. You should come over to Grumman. We're going to be on Long Island forever. They'll never go out of business, and they'll never move. We put the men on the moon. You do that for Grumman and for the U.S.A., you got your job for life, and so do your kids and your grandkids. Layoffs are out of the question. You can take that to the bank."

"Maybe I'll check it out," Pete said. "I could use a change. Things are not good at Republic."

"You should check it out," Andy said. "Grumman will *never* sell out. They'll be on Long Island forever."

"Hey, what do you guys think of this O'Hair woman and the way she's suing the government because the Apollo 8 heroes read from the Bible while they were going around the Moon last Christmas," Jake said. "It was *Christmas*, for Christ's sake!"

"It think everyone's entitled to their own opinion," Richie said.

"Always the peacemaker," Harry chuckled.

"I am a man of *love*," Richie said, bowing in jest. "Hey, this is the Sixties, right? We're all about love, love, love."

"Well, I'd *love* another shot of Fleischmann's," Harry said, pushing the shot glass toward Richie.

"A *lovely* request," Richie said, reaching for the bottle.

"I've never understood these atheists," Jake said. "Long John Nebel had her on his show. She was debating this minister. I forget his name. Doesn't matter. The bitch wouldn't let the poor guy get a word in. What a loudmouth. And she says she's going to take her case all the way to the Supreme Court. And all because our brave men read from the Bible on Christmas while they were going around and around the Moon. She says it's all about separation of church and state. My ass it is. She's a commie. I hope somebody kills her."

Richie filled beers. Said nothing.

"What do you think, Brian?" Jake said. "Huh? Let's hear what *you* have to say. You listen to Long John's show. I know you do. What do you think of this atheist bitch O'Hair?"

"She's loud," Brian said.

"But she talks nonsense," Jake said.

Brian said nothing.

"Don't you think she talks nonsense, Brian?" Jake said. "I'm asking you a question. Speak up. Don't you think she's wrong about what she says about God?"

"I don't know," Brian said. "I was just listening to the show."

"Ah, but part of being a *man* is you have to make up your own mind about things, Brian," Jake said, pointing his finger. "You need to take a stand against a bitch like that. What the hell is the matter with you, Brian? Be a *man*."

Brian said nothing.

"Brian *is* a man, Jake," Richie said, leaning in. "He became a man when his brother Sean and his father died. He's supporting his mother now. He's a *man*, Jake. Just like the rest of us in here. Don't question that."

"Hey, calm down, Richie. I was just busting the kid's balls. Just having a little fun with him."

"Leave him alone." Richie said.

"Yeah, yeah. Okay. Calm down, will ya? Don't get your balls in an uproar."

Richie wasn't smiling.

"Okay, *okay*," Jake said. "I got it. You win. Hey, Brian. Never mind."

Brian said nothing.

Show Me

Eighteen-year-old Brian was eye to eye with fifteen-year-old Hannah when she reached the bottom of her back stoop, and those eyes burned him with their intensity. She wore a white nightgown that came down to just above her knees. Her feet were long and slender, pale and bare, and she was exactly as tall as Brian.

"Show me," Hannah said. She reached out her hand and took his. Her fingers felt smooth and hard, like white tapers. They walked the length of the driveway. He shined the flashlight on the ground ahead of them.

"We don't need that," Hannah said aloud. He turned it off.

"Where are your parents?" Brian whispered.

"They're sleeping. It's very late," Hannah said. "You don't have to whisper. Everyone is asleep. It's nighttime."

"I don't want to wake them, or any of the neighbors," Brian said. "I could get in trouble for doing this."

She stopped and stared at him in the moonlight. Burned him again with those eyes. She squeezed his hand.

"No you won't," she said. "I asked you to show me the milk and the ice on your truck. You can't get into trouble for that. You just can't."

"Are you sure?" Brian said.

"Yes, I'm sure. You can't get into trouble because I asked you to do it. You must listen to me. Please."

"Okay," Brian said, feeling like she had just grown older than him by at least 20 years.

"Show me," she said, tugging his hand. *"Show me."*

She quickened their pace the rest of the way to the truck.

"Um. Here it is?" Brian said, pulling back the quilt to expose a row of iced milk.

"Yes," Hannah said. She touched the ice, and giggled. She was suddenly younger than he was. A little girl. Giggling.

"I want to touch a milk bottle to my face." She bounced three times on the balls of her feet, becoming taller than him for a moment. "Is that okay?"

"Yes," Brian said, not considering her slight acne. "Do you want me to get it for you?"

"May I get it myself? I need to touch it."

"Yes," Brian said.

She looked at the case and slowly swirled the tip of her index finger over the wet, paper caps. He said nothing.

"It's wonderful," she said.

"It is," Brian whispered.

She chose a bottle in the middle of the case and lifted it slowly. The ice slid down, making the sad sound it always made, like loss. She held the bottle in both hands and pressed it against the right side of her face.

She closed her eyes and sighed.

Then she quarter-turned the square bottle and touched it to the other side of her face. Sighed again. He watched and counted her breaths. Four. Five. Six. Her face was damp and beautiful.

She opened her eyes and handed him the bottle.

"You do it," she said. "The other two sides. Please."

He raised the bottle to his face and held it there. She watched him. Breathed. Watched.

"Now the fourth side," she said. "On the other side of your face. To complete."

He did as he was told. He was good that way.

"Can you feel the milk?" she said.

"Yes."

"And the mothers that gifted it?"

"Huh?"

"The cows. The mothers that gifted the milk. Can you feel their energy through the glass?"

"I guess," Brian said, confused.

"They're selfless."

"Huh?"

"The cows," Hannah said. "They're selfless. They give without asking for anything in return, other than more grass to eat, so that they can give more milk. Their milk is life to so many, and they give it freely."

"They're cows," Brian said.

"Yes."

"It's what cows do," Brian said. "I used to feed them grass when I was a boy and the cows were here on Long Island. I fed them the grass that I cut. From our lawn. In brown bags from the grocery store. I fed them all summer long. My mother gave me the brown bags. I fed the cows."

"Then you helped to make milk," Hannah said. "You helped to make life."

"I did?"

"Yes," Hannah said. "You did."

Brian smiled.

"Thank you," Hannah said.

"You're welcome," Brian said.

She turned and padded up her driveway, not looking back.

He stood there holding the bottle in both hands. A bit of the ice on the truck slipped and fell. Lost. The tiny sound he was so used to hearing startled him now.

Why?

He glanced at the cases of milk. And back at the house.

She was gone.

He got into the truck. Stared out the windshield. Turned the page in the route book. Let out the clutch.

Long John Nebel talked on in the endless air, wondering who *really* killed Jack Kennedy.

Brian said nothing.

Delaney's 2018

"Why do you say it's for the best that he didn't come over here?" Brian whispered.

Apple shook her head quickly, looked down the bar. He was watching FOX News.

Brian nodded. Sipped his beer.

The man finished his Bud and pushed the bottle forward.

"Another?" Apple said down the bar.

He shook his head, put money on the bar, reached for his cane, and worked his way off the stool.

"See you tomorrow?" she said.

"Good lord willing," he said without looking at Apple. He hobbled toward the door.

Brian got up to open the door for him but the man held up his free hand.

"No," he said, waving Brian away with the cane. "Sit!"

Brian went back to his stool.

"Who is he?" Brian said when the man was gone.

"He's my father," Apple said.

"Jeez, really? I thought he was just a regular."

"He *is* a regular," Apple said. "Well, at least for the past few weeks he is. He comes here in every afternoon and always at the same time. He sits where he was just sitting so he can watch FOX News with the sound off. He orders - well, he doesn't actually *order*; I just know - two Bud longnecks, no glass. He gets one right after the other, just like you saw. And he hardly talks to me, even if we're the only two people in here. He pays with cash, tips well, and then he gets up and leaves. He does this every day that I'm here, which is Monday through Friday."

"Why?"

"I suppose he's trying to make amends for all the lousy things he did to my mother and me throughout our lives."

Brian said nothing.

Apple bent and washed some pint glasses furiously. Brian looked out the window.

The Mustang hadn't returned. He knew it never would.

"Got a story you'd like to share?" Brian said when she came back to him.

"You really want to hear it?" She looked at the door.

"Sure," Brian said.

"Okay, my father. He gets into arguments. And you never know what's going to set him off. He's always been that way. He looks for fights."

"Fist fights?" Brian said.

"Not anymore," Apple said. "He used to. Just word fights these days. He'd get killed in a fistfight. You saw him."

"He's retired?"

"Yes," Apple said.

"What did he do for a living?"

"He was a police detective," Apple said. "He doesn't like people."

"I guess being a cop can do that to you," Brian said.

"No, he was like that from the start. From before he was a cop. He likes to argue, and he likes to pick on people. It doesn't matter who. It amuses him. He's a bully."

"What does he argue about?"

"About anything," Apple said. "It's his sport, and it's a nasty one. If you say you're a Republican, he'll say he's a Democrat and start a fight over current events. If you say you're a Democrat, he'll suddenly be a Republican and talk nonsense from the opposite side. If you're a Communist, he's be a Fascist. If you're a Muslim, he's a Christian. If you're a Christian, he's a Jew. He just loves fighting with people and he gets nasty and cutting. He's a bully, and I think he lives to hurt people. When he was on the job he'd sit in the bars and loud-talk. Someone who didn't know what he was up to would start in with him, maybe take a poke at him when it got real heated. And that's what my father was waiting for. He'd pull his badge, and sometimes even his gun, and arrest the guy."

"Jeez," Brian said. "That's crazy."

"It sure is, and it finally caught up with him. The job forced him into retirement. He had his twenty in and they told him he'd get his pension, but he had to leave. Losing the power of that badge and gun made him even worse."

Brian shook his head, but he said nothing.

"And now he comes in here every afternoon. To *my* place. He tells me he's a changed man and that he's going to prove it to me by coming in here every day and not getting involved in an argument or a fistfight. You saw him. You think he can fight?"

"No" Brian said.

"I don't trust him, and I like this job. I don't want him to be the cause of me losing it because he started a riot in here."

"How was he as a father?" Brian said.

"He was horrible. He put my mother in an early grave with his nonsense."

"How did she die?"

"Her heart gave out," Apple said.

"I'm sorry," Brian said.

"So that's why I'm glad he didn't join us at this end of the bar," Apple said. "He should stay down there by himself. You don't need his nonsense. Neither do I."

Brian nodded. Finished his beer.

"More?" Apple said.

"Sure. More for you?"

"What the hell," Apple said and poured for both of them.

"Are you married, Apple?"

"No!" she said. "*No, no, no.*" She held out her left hand, palm down. For the first time, Brian noticed that she had a small tattoo on the top of her ring finger. It read, NO! in blue ink.

"Wow," Brian said. "That's pretty definite."

"So far, so good," Apple said and sipped her wine.

Daddy

Stewart Kepler's daddy, Leonard, was born in 1907. He was a tailor, and a supervisor in a factory that made Army uniforms. During World War 2, the government considered his job essential to the war effort, so he was exempt from the draft, constantly near uniforms, but never actually in one.

When peace arrived, he saw opportunity in a new concept called the coin-laundry business. Most Americans had been scrubbing their clothes on washboards in bathtubs before the war, so this new coin-laundry thing captivated them. For just a few dimes you could have a machine do all the work for you. It was a time-saving wonder to them and people flocked to them.

Leonard Kepler had made good money during the war years and he had invested much of it. He built his first coin laundry in 1947 when the Long Island housing market was starting to boom.

Most of those new houses, such as the 17,000 William Levitt was building on the Hempstead Plain, included washing machines, but not clothes dryers. What caught Leonard Kepler's attention was that William Levitt, the grandson of a rabbi, wouldn't sell to either Jews or African Americans. He said this was just good business because he believed that if he sold even one house to a member of either minority, the majority of white people would not buy his houses. And that was okay with the government back then. It was just business. Nothing personal.

So those who got left out of Levitt's whites-only, Levittown neighborhood, rented apartments in Long Island's older neighborhoods, and hardly any of those apartments had washing machines. Leonard Kepler opened his first coin laundry in one of those neighborhoods because he knew that good people, regardless of race or religion, want clean clothes, and like Frank Winfield Woolworth before him, Leonard Kepler recognized that if you sell something people need for just a dime, the dimes will quickly grow into dollars, and lots of them.

Leonard Kepler did very well.

By the spring of 1953, when his son, Stewart, married Madeline Cohen, Leonard Kepler owned five laundromats, and each was a beautiful cash machine. Tons of dimes slid through his machines and into Leonard's pockets, and most of them out of the sight of the IRS.

It was Leonard Kepler's American dream, but wide awake and stretching.

However, happy stories often have sad parts.

Leonard Kepler always emptied the money from his washers, dryers, and vending machines between 3 A.M. and 5 A.M. because, even though Leonard's Coin Laundries never closed, this was the hour when business was slowest and most people were asleep. Leonard liked to do his business when other people weren't watching.

"We make money even when we sleep," he told his wife, Bernice. Bernice smiled and laughed with him whenever he said that, and he said it often. It was the family motto. Leonard was a good provider.

On December 10, 1953, he was raking the dimes out of clothes dryer No. 9 in Coin Laundry No. 3 when his heart spasmed and smacked him to the black linoleum floor. No one else was there to help. It was 3:15 A.M. He passed out of this world 15 minutes later, surrounded by loose change.

Leelannee Beasley found him at 7 A.M. that morning when she came into the coin laundry with her three-year-old son, Joshua, and a sack of dirty laundry. She screamed, covered Joshua's eyes, and called the police from Leonard Kepler's pay phone. She used her own dime and was never reimbursed.

Bernice, who was now the sole owner, had a situation. All of this coin-laundry business had been Leonard's concern. Her job had been to spend the money her husband made for her, which she did very well.

Her son, Stewart, who had never wanted to work for his father because he thought his father was too stern and demanding, instantly offered to quit his job as a State Farm insurance salesman on a lousy commission, and run the coin-laundry business for his mother full-time, knowing he was her heir when she passed, which perhaps would be soon. After all, she was grieving and under a lot of stress. One can only hope.

Bernice smiled and said yes, yes, of course, and Stewart went happily to work providing for his mother's needs and skimming generously for himself.

Hannah arrived a year later, and not at the most convenient time, but as Stewart said to his wife, Madeline, "Accidents happen. What can you do?"

Stewart had opened two more coin laundries, and was now looking to buy into a bowling alley, another cash-only business.

Madeline was going to business each day at her salon, Teasin' & Pleasin', yet another beautiful cash business. She had taken courses in high school that taught her how to cut and color hair, do permanent waves, manicures and pedicures, but she performed none of these services now. Her staff of six young women did all the work. Madeline had groomed one of these women, Gabina Aguirre, to manage the place when she and Stewart began traveling more to relieve their stress.

"How do you know she won't steal from you?" Stewart had said before their first trip to Europe.

"How do you know Francisco won't steal from *you*?" Madeline said. Francisco fixed the laundry machines and collected the dimes when Stewart couldn't.

"Because if he did I would call Immigration and have him and everyone in his family deported. He knows that," Stewart said.

"I can do the same," Madeline said. "None of my ladies are supposed to be here, and neither are their children. It's a good balance. They understand what I would do to them if they tried to steal from me. They fear me."

"Fear is motivational," Stewart said.

"Yes, it is," Madeline said. "And we're doing very, very well."

"Yes, we are," Stewart said.

The Hannah problem, however, persisted.

"I have an idea," Stewart said one day. "Let's get an au pair to watch the baby day and night so we can go to business and not have to change diapers or do any of the other nonsense. We won't have to pay an au pair much because she'll be a poor, immigrant girl. We'll find an illegal Irish one. The Irish are good with babies. They have so many of them. That's about all they're good for. She'll be happy just to live in our fine home and take whatever we offer her."

"Where will we get her?" Madeline said.

"I've got a man in Brooklyn," Stewart said. "He has connections. Leave it to me."

Madeline clapped her manicured hands in delight.

Twenty-year-old, Maeve O'Brien with her riot of warrior-red hair, slender waist, and green eyes that flashed both promise and menace, arrived in Plainview, Long Island by way of Northern Ireland and Brooklyn, NY. Stewart had picked her up at the Brooklyn YWCA on Sunday morning, after his man had made the arrangements. Stewart thought they had gotten a great deal. She would take care of Hannah and clean the house six days a week, all for just $40 a week cash money, plus room and board. No paperwork whatsoever.

He showed Maeve her small room in the basement of their split-level house, and explained her responsibilities. Maeve listened, nodded, and did not once blink. He then walked her upstairs to the crib, where Maeve was immediately taken with tiny, sweet Hannah and her wide-set, blue eyes. Maeve bent and touched the palm of her hand to Hannah's head.

"Child," she said. "I'm Maeve. I'm here to care for you and to make of you a strong woman. How are ye?"

Stewart stood behind her.

Maeve reached down and gathered Hannah into her strong, young arms. Lifted her. Cooed over her. Didn't turn around.

Stewart stood behind Maeve, staring at her behind.

He bit his lower lip.

Madeline was off watching women getting their hair colored.

On Tuesday morning, Madeline drove Maeve O'Brien back to the Brooklyn YWCA. They didn't speak along the way. Stewart was home with Hannah, nursing his broken jaw.

Madeline thought Maeve's vicious left-hook answer to Stewart's alleged groping was uncalled for. And besides, if Maeve didn't expect to be admired, she should not have shown up at their home looking so beautiful. She should have known that boys will be boys. Shame on her.

A series of nannies followed, none of them younger than sixty, and none of them under 200 pounds. None, however, stayed longer than two months. Each found the Kepler's arrogance and conceit more than they could bear.

But nevertheless, the Keplers managed to ratchet Hannah's young life far enough forward to where they could finally plug her into a nearby, full-day program that could, when necessary because of the Kepler's business obligations, also stretch into early evenings, albeit at an additional cost. Stewart and Madeline cringed at the expense of this program, but they did, after all, have to go to business. That was paramount, and people would just have to understand.

And so Hannah grew.

Route 2

Brian walked quickly to the back of the Kepler house, milk in hands and not sure what to do when he got there. Should he just put the milk in the box, grab the empties, and leave? Or should he stand there and wait for something to happen? But what could happen?

He broke into a run and slalomed around the corner of the house.

Hannah was sitting on the stoop, her long left arm on the milk box, her hair wild. She wore black shorts, a black tee shirt, and white tennis shoes. No socks.

"I want to ride with you tonight," she said.

"How far?" Brian said, not believing he had just said that.

"How far am I allowed?"

"You're not allowed at all," Brian said, shaking his head. "Not allowed. No. At least I don't think you're allowed."

"Did someone tell you I'm not allowed?" Hannah said.

"No."

"Then how do you know I'm not allowed?"

"I don't," Brian said.

"Then to how many houses may I ride with you tonight?"

"Five?" Brian said.

"How about ten?" Hannah said.

"Um, okay," Brian said. "But don't tell anyone, okay?"

"Who would I tell?" Hannah said. "My parents are sleeping."

"Do they know you're awake and dressed and outside? Do they know you want to ride in a milk truck?"

"They're sleeping," Hannah said.

"Um, okay then," Brian said. "I guess it's okay."

"Let me have those," Hannah said, reaching for the milk. "Please."

He handed them to her.

"I'll be right back. Stay here."

Brian nodded. Three times.

She brought the bottles into the house. He was holding the three empties when she came back out.

"Please let me hold those," she said, reaching for the empties. "Show me how you do it."

Brian took her hand and spread her fingers wide. He placed the necks of two empty bottles between her fingers, and the third empty across her palm. "That's how we do it," he said. "You have good fingers for this. They're long and strong."

Hannah wiggled the fingers on her free hand and nodded. "Yes," she said. "They are." She took his hand with that one and they walked to the truck.

"They go here," Brian said, pointing at the empty spaces in a crate.

She put them there.

They stood on the side of the truck, looking at the crate with the empties. Neither spoke.

"Now what?" she said after a minute.

"Oh. Well, um, you can't drive the truck," Brian whispered. "I have to do that. You're not allowed to drive the truck."

"That's okay," Hannah said aloud. "I don't know how to drive. I'm fifteen."

She walked around the truck to the passenger side and got in.

"Fifteen?" Brian said, still standing in the road.

"Yes. Fifteen," Hannah said. "Get in."

Brian did as he was told

"Where do we go now?" Hannah said.

Brian looked in the route book.

"Just four blocks," he said. "We go to Rosen next. Do you know Rosen?"

"Yes," Hannah said. "What do they get?"

"They get four quarts of whole milk."

"Okay," Hannah said.

"I've never met Rosen," Brian said. "I just see their milk box. I hardly ever meet anybody because it's nighttime. They're all sleeping. Most of them are. It's nighttime. Sometimes some of them ask for something that's not on their order, but most of the time they're all sleeping."

"The parents are nice," Hannah said. "But their daughter is mean to me."

"Who?"

"Rosen," Hannah said. "Sarah Rosen."

"What does she do to you? How is she mean to you?"

"She calls me Olive Oyl," Hannah said.

"Like the cartoon?" Brian said.

"Yes."

"Why do you think that's mean?" Brian said.

"It's how she says it," Hannah said.

"I don't understand."

"She says it to try to make me feel sad. She says it in a nasty way. Other kids do that too. It's because I'm tall and skinny. That's why they call me Olive Oyl. Olive Oyl is tall and skinny.

Like me. We have the same color hair." Hannah touched her black hair. "I don't have any friends."

"I think Olive Oyl is beautiful," Brian said. "She's so kind. She helps Popeye take care of Swee'Pea. Did you know someone left Swee'Pea on Popeye's doorstep? Popeye adopted him. That was a kind thing to do. He didn't have to do that, but he did. Olive Oyl helps him take care of Swee'Pea. And she is always trying to make peace between Popeye and Bluto."

"But Popeye and Bluto fight anyway," Hannah said.

"Yes, they do. They do." Brian nodded furiously. "But there's a happy ending to it, Hannah, because Olive Oyl married Popeye and they lived happily ever after with Swee'Pea. Forever and ever. It's true. It's a good story. A happy story. You can watch it on the TV. Olive Oyl is a beautiful person. You shouldn't feel bad if they call you by her name. Really. Olive Oyl is *wonderful*."

"I don't have any friends," Hannah said again.

"Do you want me to be your friend?" Brian said.

Hannah looked at her long fingers and twined them together. "Maybe. We'll see."

"Here we are at Rosen," Brian said.

"What do we do now?"

"Come. I'll show you.

They got out of the truck and Brian pulled back the quilt.

"The whole milk is here." He pointed. "It has these caps. That's how you can tell them from the skim milk. The color of the ink is different. Blue is whole; red is skim. See?" Hannah nodded. "The skim milk is over there." Brian pointed. "Take out four bottles of these," he said, touching the blue caps of the whole milk.

"Can I touch the ice first?"

"Sure, touch it all you'd like. Put some in your mouth if you want to. I do that all the time, especially in the summer. Just eat one chip at a time, though. If you put too many pieces in your mouth you'll get a spiky headache."

"Okay," Hannah said. She chose a piece of ice and put it in her mouth. She giggled with her tongue out and Brian suddenly felt like he was standing there with a five-year-old rather than a 15-year-old. He wondered how she does that.

Hannah reached for the four bottles and Brian showed her where to place them in the carrier to balance the weight.

"Can I do it with just my hands?" Hannah said.

"If you want to, sure. But let's do it that way on the next stop so you'll get good at both ways. The next house also gets four bottles."

"You're a good teacher," Hannah said.

Brian smiled.

"Let's go," she said.

They held hands and walked to the milk box on the front stoop. Brian lit the way with his flashlight. There wasn't a cobblestone on top of the box, which was a good thing. Maybe he'd tell Hannah about the trapped cat that scared him. He wasn't sure if he should, though. He'd have to wait and see.

"Take out the empties and put the full ones in," Brian whispered. She did. "Good job. Okay, let's go back to the truck."

They held hands again.

They did the next two houses without much conversation as Brian drove, mostly because Brian wasn't completely sure how to talk to a girl, and Hannah was listening to Long John Nebel on the truck's radio. The topic tonight was witchcraft.

"What happened to the other man?" Hannah said when they got to the Johnson house and were getting the milk out of the ice.

"What other man?" Brian said.

"The old man who used to bring our milk. I haven't seen him in a long time. Where did he go?"

"That's Ole Olson. He taught me how to do all of this." Brian gestured around the truck.

"What happened to him?"

"He died," Brian said.

"When?"

"Last March."

"How?"

"He got a bad bellyache on Christmas last year. It happened when we were doing the milk. He was real sick. I took him to the hospital. The one in Plainview. Plainview Hospital." Brian nodded three times. "I finished the route all by myself for the first time that night. I was alone. I did it all by myself. It was Christmas."

"Did you see Santa?" Hannah said.

"No."

"What was the bellyache from?" Hannah said.

"It was his gallbladder. They took it out and everyone thought he was going to be okay, but then something happened to the inside of his head. To his brain. They call it a stroke. He couldn't move this side of his body anymore." Brian tapped his right side. "And then it got worse. Much worse. And he couldn't move the other side either. And then he got a coma and just died. In March. It was a cold day when he died. It was real sad. I cried."

Brian went quiet.

"Do you know where his energy went?" Hannah said.

Brian looked at Hannah.

"What do you mean?"

"His energy," Hannah whispered. "Do you know? Do you? Could you feel it move?"

"*What do you mean?*"

"His *energy*. Energy never goes away; it just moves around. Did you feel where it went? Can you feel it now? Be still and feel for it."

"I don't know how to do this," Brian said. "I've never tried to do this."

"Be still," Hannah said. "Shh."

"I don't think I know how to be still," Brian said. "I move all the time. When I do the milk, I move all the time. I'm never still."

"Shh. It's okay," Hannah said. She put her hands on his cheeks. Her hands were cold from the ice. "Shh."

Brian took three deep breaths.

"That's good," Hannah said. "Be still"

Brian quieted.

She moved her long fingers over his eyes.

"Shh. Remember for me. Was he a good man? Remember him. Tell me about him. Was he a *good* man?"

"Yes, he was a *very* good man," Brian said, his eyes closed under her long, cold fingers that felt so soothing. "He was good to me and to my mother. He bought me new shoes when I couldn't afford them, and he bought me breakfast every night. An apple turnover and black coffee. It tasted so good. And he told me stories, and he taught me how to do the milk, and he paid me well so that I could help my mother with the bills. He was a *very* good man. Yes, he was. I miss him a lot." He choked back a sob.

"Shh," Hannah said. She slowly took her hands away from his face. "Open your eyes." He did.

"His energy went to a *beautiful* place," Hannah said, nodding and smiling. "A *better* place." Her eyes grew wide. "Better. *Much* better." She smiled.

"Where did it go?"

"What did Ole Olson want most of all in this world?" Hannah said. "What would have made him the most happy?"

Brian blushed.

"Do you know was it was?" Hannah said. "What he wanted most?"

"I think so, but I don't want to say it," Brian said.

Hannah waited.

Waited.

"Is it a secret?" she whispered.

"Not really a *secret*. He talked to everyone about it. I just don't want to say it. It's embarrassing."

"You'll feel better if you do," Hannah said. "I'll be able to tell you where his energy went if you share with me. It will be to a wonderful place. You'll see."

Brian said nothing. Hannah waited.

"Are you ready to tell me now?"

"Yes."

"What did he want more than *anything* in the world?" Hannah said.

"Um, he wanted, a roomful of, um. . . ladies' breasts," Brian said.

"Did he say *why* he wanted a roomful of ladies' breasts?" Hannah said.

"He said they were beautiful and he just wanted to feel them," Brian said, embarrassed. "He said they were like soft throw pillows. It was his dream to have a roomful of them. He wanted to take off his shirt and his pants and roll around in them."

"I know where his energy is," Hannah giggled. "I can feel it." Her wet hands touched her chest. "I can feel it here."

"Where?" Brian said, watching her hands move.

"His energy went into the Wonderbra factory. It will travel all over the world with their products. That's better than just one roomful of ladies' breasts. He's close to millions of ladies' breasts now. All shapes, and sizes, and colors. All ages. All soft and beautiful. All loving him because he loved them in this life. That's where he is now. His energy is fully there. I feel it."

Brian laughed and sobbed, and all at the same time.

And then Hannah smiled, which, to Brian, was like watching dawn.

She took his hands in hers.

And she smiled.

"That's ten houses," Brian said when they reached that point. "I have to get you back home now."

"Why?"

"Because I don't know if I'm supposed to be doing this with you, even though you told me where Ole's energy is now."

"Okay, but how about just one more house?" Hannah said. "Please?" She smiled.

"I don't know," Brian said. "This next house is the Weinreich house. It's very scary there."

"Why is it very scary?"

"They have a big dog."

"I like dogs," Hannah said.

"This one is the Hound of the Baskervilles," Brian said.

"Show me," Hannah said.

"You sure?"

"Yes."

"Okay."

Brian put six quarts of whole milk into the carrier and grabbed a dozen eggs from the miscellaneous crate.

"I'll carry the milk. You carry the eggs," he said. "Try not to drop them when Klaus runs at us."

"Who is Klaus?" Hannah said.

"Their dog. He's a big German shepherd. He's on a chain. He's vicious."

"That's sad, being on a chain," Hannah said. "I wouldn't want to be on a chain. Would you?"

"No," Brian said.

"That's why Klaus is angry. He needs help and he's not getting it. We can help him."

"What do you mean?"

"Let's go. I'll show you."

She took his free hand and they walked to the backyard.

When they made the turn, Klaus ran at them without barking, as he always did. The chain played out and brought him up short. He gagged, as he always did, and then he clambered up onto his hind legs, snarling and pawing the air between them as he strained against his collar. He never barked.

"See what I mean?" Brian whispered. "But we can get to the milk box. He can't go that far."

Hannah didn't answer. She let go of Brian's hand and handed him the dozen eggs.

144

"What are you doing?" Brian whispered. Hannah said nothing. She stood very still and her lips began to move silently, as if in prayer. To Brian's astonishment, Klaus stopped snarling. His eyes were locked on Hannah's wide-set, blue eyes. He quieted.

She reached out with both hands.

Klaus sat.

"What's happening?" Brian whispered. Hannah said nothing. She walked to the dog and took his face in both of her hands. Brian cringed but he said nothing. Klaus whimpered. Hannah unhooked the chain from his collar.

"Are you crazy?" Brian whispered. "He's going to *kill* us."

"Shh," Hannah said. Brian wasn't sure if she was talking to him or to the dog.

Klaus licked Hannah's hands. She went down on her knees and hugged him like a child. He licked her face.

"What's *happening*?" Brian whispered.

"Shhh," Hannah said.

She stood. Klaus lay down at her feet.

"He said he wanted the chain off," Hannah said. "He said it hurts him."

"What do you mean he *said*. I didn't hear him say anything. Dogs can't talk."

"Were you listening?" Hannah said, looking at Klaus, not at Brian.

"Dogs can't talk," Brian said again.

"If you listen, animals *will* talk to you," Hannah said. "But you have to be very quiet and very still to hear them. You have to respect who they are if you want them to respect who you are. That's what I just did. Klaus knew I wanted to help him and he told me he wouldn't hurt me or you, and that he doesn't want to leave this house. He just doesn't want to be chained anymore. It hurts him. None of us want to be chained."

"But we can't leave him unchained," Brian said.

"Yes, we can," Hannah said. "He'll stay here."

"How do you know?"

"He told me so," Hannah said. "He promised."

"But what happens when the Weinreichs wake up and see that he's not chained. I'm going to be in trouble for that," Brian said. "They'll know it was me who did it."

"But it wasn't you who did it. It was me," Hannah said.

"You know what I mean. I'm the milkman. I'm the only one who's supposed to be back here in the middle of the night with him." He pointed at Klaus, calm and on the ground at Hannah's feet, breathing softly.

"Don't worry. He told me you won't be in trouble. He won't run away. He likes the Weinreichs. He likes living here. He just doesn't like the chain in the night. They'll see tomorrow morning that he doesn't need the chain. That he will stay here and protect them without it. We can go now."

"But what if they chain him again?" Brian said.

She put the empties into the carrier and took Brian by the hand.

"Then we'll unchain him again," she said. "We can go now. You can take me home now. Thank you for caring about him. He's okay now. See?" She turned and smiled.

The dog was standing and wagging his tail.

When Brian pulled up in front of the Kepler house he realized that in the two nights they had been together he had never told Hannah his name. She was getting out of the truck when he said, "Do you want to know my name?"

"I know your name," she said without turning around.

"You do?"

"Yes."

"What is it?"

She turned and leaned in.

"Popeye," she giggled like a five-year-old. "That's your name, and next time we'll do *15* houses."

She skipped up the driveway and into her backyard.

Fifteen

"How *old* is this girl?" Richie said.

"Fifteen," Brian said.

"Heck of a thing to wake me up with, Brian."

"Sorry," Brian said. "I didn't want to talk about it in front of the guys at the bar."

"Yeah, I get that," Richie said. "There are some ball busters in there and I'm sure they'd have a lot to say about it. You did the right thing coming to me. Just give me a second to get my head together here, okay?"

"Okay."

Richie stretched, and unscrewed the lid of the Tropicana orange-juice bottle. He took a sip and set the bottle on the ground next to the Mustang.

"So tell me, and go slow," he said, gesturing with the wide bottle cap. "Slow, please. Where did you meet this young lady?"

"On Route Two. She's a customer's daughter. Her name is . . ."

"Wait!" he said, holding up the cap like it was a badge. "Please don't tell me her name."

"Why not?"

"It's better that I don't know," Richie said. He bent, picked up the bottle. Took a longer sip and replaced the cap. Set it back down.

Brian watched him.

"So she's a customer's kid and she's fifteen," Richie said, wiping his mouth with the back of his hand. "Okay. I got that. And *then* what happened?"

"She rode with me in the milk truck," Brian said.

"Oh, jeez. How *far*?"

"We went to eleven houses after her house," Brian said.

"Why?"

"Because she wanted to."

"And you went along with that?"

"Yes."

"Why?"

"Because she asked," Brian said.

"Brian, you're eighteen."

"Yes."

"And *then* what happened?" Richie said. "Tell me *everything*."

"Um, I brought her back to her house."

"That all that happened?" Richie said.

"Yes."

"Did you go *into* her house?"

"No," Brian said. "Why would I do that?"

Richie stared hard at Brian.

"Did you touch her?"

"Yes."

"Sweet Jesus," Richie said, shaking his head. "*Where* did you touch her?"

"I touched her in the driveways mostly," Brian said. "It was dark."

"*Which* driveways?

150

"The milk customers' driveways," Brian said. "It was dark. She doesn't like flashlights. She was afraid we would fall, so we held hands. That's how I touched her."

"Oh," Richie said. "Did you touch anything else, or just her hands in the driveways?"

"We touched the milk bottles," Brian said. "The full ones and the empty ones. And the milk carrier. We both touched that. Both of us. Oh, and the ice. We touched the ice. And we ate some of it."

"Did you touch *her*, Brian. Did you touch her *body*?"

"Just her hands," Brian said.

"Okay, that's good," Richie said. "She's underage, you know, Brian."

"What does that mean?"

"She's under sixteen. If you touch her you could go to jail."

"She touched my face!" Brian said.

"Did you touch her back when she touched your face?"

"No. I just touched her hands when we were walking," Brian said. "She wanted to hold hands and she wanted to hold my face when she talked to me about Ole Olson and his energy. That's all. Am I in trouble, Richie?"

"Not if you just did what you say you did. Not yet, anyway. Listen, I gotta ask you this straight out, did you touch her in a sexual way? Tell me the truth."

"You mean like kissing?" Brian said.

"No," Richie said. "Not like kissing. Like *more* than kissing."

"No!" Brian said, recoiling a step backward into the road. Richie grabbed Brian's arm and looked quickly left and right. No cars were coming. It was still early.

"Watch what you're doing with the road, okay?" Richie said.

Brian was shaking. "I'm sorry," he said. "I'm sorry."

"It's okay," Richie said. "Brian, listen to me. It's good that you didn't touch this girl in a too-friendly way. Let's keep it like that for now, okay? If you touch this girl in a too-friendly way, even if she asks you to do that, you could go to jail for twenty years."

"But I would *never* touch her like that," Brian said. "That's for married people." Tears were welling in his eyes. *"Never!"*

"Then why are we talking, Brian? I'm not a lawyer but I've always heard that fifteen will get you twenty," Richie said. "I don't know if it's true, but I've always heard it."

"What does that mean?"

"It means that if the girl is fifteen and you're eighteen, and you do a sex thing with her, you can go to jail for twenty years. Fifteen gets you twenty."

Brian said nothing. He was shaking.

"What do you want from me, Brian? What are you *really* asking me?"

"I'm asking if her and me should be friends? She doesn't have any friends, Richie. I think she wants her and me to be friends. A lot of people her age are mean to her. The people in her school. They call her Olive Oyl."

"What's wrong with Olive Oyl?"

"I don't know. I like Olive Oyl," Brian said.

"Who doesn't like Olive Oyl?" Richie said.

"Should her and me be friends, Richie? That's what I want to ask you. Should we be friends? Is it okay?"

"Yes, it's okay, Brian. But be careful with her. She's fragile. She's a child. Don't do anything other than hold her hand, okay? You got enough stuff going on in your life right now. You don't need that sort of girl problem."

"Okay," Brian said. He nodded. Three times.

"Okay. You good now, Brian?"

"Yes. I think so."

"Okay. Listen, I gotta get home for a couple of hours. Stop by the bar this afternoon if you can. We'll talk more then if you need to talk more. Up to you. Okay? We'll talk in private if you need to. I promise. Okay?"

"Okay. I have to switch route books and get the oil changed first."

"Good, Brian. You go do that. Maybe I'll see you later."

Brian watched the Mustang leap away from him. It was like it had a life of its own. So much energy. Maybe the Mustang had its own opinion about all of this. He wondered what Hannah would say about the Mustang.

Brian watched it go.

Mae Olson

Mae Olson answered the door, still in her robe. She hadn't tied it closed and he could see her sheer nightgown. He looked at the floor. She smelled sour.

"Well, look who ish," she slurred, standing aside and gesturing him in with an outstretched arm. "Come in. Come."

"Good morning, Mrs. Olson." Brian held out the route book. The cash he had collected from the milk boxes was tucked into the customers' pages.

"Ish it still morning?" Mae said and hiccuped.

Brian looked at his watch. It was 11:30. Mae grabbed his hand and turned his wrist toward her so she could see for herself.

"I supo ish," Mae said, answering her own question. She turned, still holding his hand and walked toward the kitchen. "Come," she said.

"If we can just swap route books now I can be on my way," Brian said.

"Nah so fass, nah so fass," Mae slurred. "I needa see what you got fa me. Come."

He looked at the floor and followed. She still had his hand in her grip.

"How mush money did you gemme?" she said, letting go of his hand. She sat at the dining-room table and opened the route book.

"I don't count it, Mrs. Olson. You know that. I just pick up the envelopes from the milk boxes and put them into the route book. I don't know how much it is today, or any other day. I'll just take the other route book and go now. Thank you. I'll go. Thank you." He reached for the book.

"No, no. *Here*. Sit," she said, patting the chair to her right. "Nest to me. Itch better dis way. I have questions about how *mush* money."

Brian hesitated.

"*Here!*" she smacked the chair. "Sit."

Brian sat.

"Thach better," she said, patting his thigh. "Mush, mush better." She squeezed his thigh. Her hand moved.

Brian shifted his legs away from her.

"Was wrong?" she slurred. "Was wrong! Sip still!"

"Mrs. Olson. Can we just swap books now? All your money is in the book there." He pointed at the route book. "You can count it for yourself. I need to get the oil changed on the truck today. I have to go now." He slid off the side of the chair. She reached for his leg again and fell across the chair and onto the floor under the table. She banged her head on the table leg. Her robe was wide open, her legs akimbo.

"Whoops!" she said and giggled. "Looka me now. Wooo! All good to go!" She got halfway up and then slid down again. "Help me. Help me up," she said, reaching for him.

Brian bent and reached for her hands. He pulled her to her feet. She pressed herself into him. "Thas better," she slurred, reaching for his crotch.

"I have to go, Mr. Olson," Brian said, pushing her back.

"Whasa rush?" she said. "We got time." She reached for him again. He stepped back.

"I really *don't* have time, Mrs. Olson. I have to get the oil changed. I have an appointment. The guys at the garage are waiting for me. I told them I had to stop here first to switch route books. They know where I am. If I'm late they're going to wonder what took me so long. And my mother needs me. My *mother* knows where I am."

"We wone take long," Mae said, stumbling into him. Brian turned sideways and she fell again. "Na soooo long. Stay and maybe I'll give you a raise. A raise." She looked at his crotch from the floor and giggled. "Raise." She held up a stiff index finger. "*Raise*. Get it?"

"I'm sorry Mrs. Olson. I have to go," Brian said.

Brian picked up the Route 1 book from the table and hurried toward the front door.

"A lady in her prime guess lonely sometime," she slurred from the floor. "Come back tomorrow and bring me my money, boy. And maybe something elsh." She laughed.

But Brian didn't hear her. He was gone.

Delaney's
2018

"When did you get the tattoo?" Brian said, pointing at her left ring finger.

"When I turned eighteen," Apple said. "That was the earliest I could do it without my dear father's permission."

"You knew then?" Brian said.

"I did."

"For sure?"

"Absolutely," Apple said.

"And sure enough to make it permanent," Brian said.

"Nothing is permanent," Apple said.

"Well, tattoos are close enough to permanent."

"I suppose. Do you have any?"

"No," Brian said.

"Why not?"

"Anything I ever felt strongly enough about that could have been tattoo-worthy didn't last," Brian said.

Apple sipped wine from her mug. Nodded.

"It's good, isn't it?" Brian said. "Drinking in the afternoon."

She smiled. "It's good."

"Good."

"Tell me a *happy* story," Apple said.

"About what?"

"The old days."

"You mean when I was a milkman?"

"Younger. In the Fifties. What was it like then?" Apple said.

"Ah, when I was a lad," Brian chuckled. "Those were also crazy times. They had us practicing ducking under our desks in school to avoid the atomic bomb. They showed us this film with a cartoon character called Bert the Turtle. If we saw the big flash outside, we were supposed to duck and cover, just like Bert did. He popped into his shell. We were supposed to put a coat or a newspaper over our head to keep from getting burned by the blast. And then, when it was safe again, we were supposed to get up and brush off the radioactivity." He brushed his hands on his shirt. "It was all so simple then."

"And then you'd just go about your business?" Apple said.

"Yes, we'd go outside and bury our dead. Oh, and it was also very important that we listen to the grown-ups for further advice."

"Did you buy that?"

"Nope."

"Good," Apple said. "But I asked for a *happy* story."

"Right," Brian said. "So let me tell you about the ice-cream men."

"Ooo," Apple said.

"We had two of them. First there was Ronnie The Pied Piper."

"The Pied Piper?"

"That was the name on his truck. Pied Piper Ice Cream."

"Sounds like a pedophile," Apple said.

"This was a more innocent time, Miss Apple. Bear with me."

"Sorry. Please continue."

"Ronnie was a clean-cut guy. He drove a white truck that was the size of a pickup and he had to climb in and out of it to get at the ice cream. It wasn't like a Mister Softee truck where the guy makes the ice cream inside and hands it out to the kids. Ronnie had to keep climbing in and out."

"Just like a milkman," Apple said.

"That never occurred to me, but yes. Thanks."

"You're welcome. I hate that Mr. Softee jingle."

"Who doesn't?"

"But about Ronnie the pedophile," Apple said.

"Yes, Ronnie," Brian said. "He wore this change holder on his belt. He'd press these levers for quarters, nickels, dimes, and pennies to make change for us. He thumbed that thing like Wyatt Earp thumbed his six-shooter. I'll never forget that. I wanted one of those. It was a mechanical marvel."

"You are a man of simple needs," Apple said.

"I am!"

"That's a good way to be."

Brian smiled.

"Did Ronnie come around every day?" Apple said.

"Yes, and pretty much at the same time all summer long. It was always after dinner, which made it perfect. He'd come down the block, pulling this rope inside the truck's cab to ring a bunch of bells mounted outside on the top of the cab. It was real low-tech and it worked like a charm. We'd come running whenever we'd hear it."

"The Pied Piper," Apple said.

"Exactly."

"What was your favorite ice cream?"

"Actually, it wasn't ice cream. I loved the Italian ices," Brian said.

"Those are nice," Apple leaned in on her elbows and smiled.

161

"We'd scoop down the center of the ice with the wooden spoon Ronnie gave us, and then we'd flip the ice over to get at the syrupy part down there at the bottom. The lemon ices were the best. And Ronnie gave us a small coupon each time we bought from him. They were the size of a business card. He made them with construction paper and a rubber stamp. If you collected ten of those cards you got a free ice cream."

"Maybe we should do that here," Apple laughed.

"It would be like the buy-backs they used to do when this place was The Landing Strip," Brian said. "Every fourth beer was on the house. No coupons required in those days."

"Those days are over," Apple laughed. "Just ask my boss."

Brian put his right hand over his heart and sighed. "So sad," he said.

"Who was the other ice-cream guy?" Apple said, still laughing. "You said there were two."

"That would be Eddie. No last name. Just Eddie. He was a greaser. You know what I mean?"

"Brylcreem, tight jeans, and leather jacket?" Apple said.

"Exactly. And an unfiltered Camel that never went out hanging off his lip. He was the anti-Pied Piper. The tough kids bought from Eddie. He was the Jerry Lee Lewis of ice-cream men. I think he even scared the cops."

"And Ronnie The Pied Piper? What musician would he have been?"

"I'd say Pat Boone," Brian said. "He was always looking over his shoulder for Eddie. I think he was afraid of him."

"I see a problem coming," Apple said.

"Yeah," Brian said. "Us Ronnie kids had to duck into the bushes when Eddie came by, especially if we were holding Ronnie The Pied Piper ice cream."

"Duck and cover," Apple said.

"Yep."

"Did Eddie give coupons for free ice-cream?"

"No, Eddie didn't have to give coupons. He just scared his kids into buying from him. If he caught them even looking at Ronnie The Pied Piper, he'd chase them with his truck."

"You're not serious," Apple said, raising her eyebrows.

"I'm not, but work with me on this," Brian said. "It makes the story better."

"Okay," Apple said. "Never let the truth get in the way of a good story. I'm with you. Did Eddie have tinkly bells on his truck?"

"No. He just had loud pipes. Eddie didn't tinkle. He meant business. Buy or die."

"What did those guys do during the winters?"

"They drove oil trucks and made deliveries to the houses. Just about everyone heated with oil back then. Ronnie and Eddie would do the ice cream in the summer and the oil in the winter. Ronnie delivered oil to our house. He looked miserable during the winter. He made like he didn't know me if I came outside when he was pumping the oil. It was like he was two different people."

"No coupons for the oil, right?" Apple said.

"Right. My father was all about turning the thermostat down, not up."

"Did Eddie deliver to the greaser-kids' houses?" Apple said.

"Now you're asking too many questions," Brian laughed.

"Well, you started it," she said.

"I did."

"Tell me more. I love this story."

"Well, there were other delivery guys, too. We had a Dugan guy who came to the house with bread and cake, and even potato chips. They went out of business in '67."

"Dugan?"

"Yeah. They drove the same sort of boxy trucks some of the milkmen drove. They're called Divcos."

"I guess the supermarkets put Dugan out of business?" Apple said. "Just like the milkmen."

Brian nodded. "We also had a beer man. He brought two cases of Ballantine Ale in refillable bottles to our back door every week."

"Wow," Apple said. "For your father?"

"For my mother."

"Really?"

"Yes. She had to put up with my father."

"I get that."

"Oh, and there was a potato-chip guy, too," Brian said. "Charles Chips. They came in these huge metal cans. The guy would bring them right to your door."

"Sounds fattening."

"Most everything was in those days," Brian said. "There was also a sharpener guy who rolled slowly through the neighborhood clanging a bell. He'd sharpen your knives, scissors, lawnmower blades, axes, machetes, scythes, sickles, switchblades, or any other murder weapon you may have in your house. Anything that needed a razor's edge, that guy would take care of it."

"Sounds deadly," Apple said.

"Not as deadly as the Fuller Brush man. He sold brooms and mops and dustpans and whatnot. That guy could bore a kid to death."

"And all this came right to your door," Apple said.

"Yep. It was the Amazon.com of its day."

"That's funny," Apple said, smiling.

"Oh, and there were other guys who drove these trucks that had kiddy rides attached to them. A small Ferris wheel, or a whip, or a big seesaw that held twenty or so screaming kids. It was nice except when someone's fingers got sliced off in the machinery."

"Yes, but didn't the doctors also make house calls back then?" Apple said.

"They did," Brian said. "They'd sew the fingers right back on."

"So there you go. No worries at all."

"It was a simpler time," Brian said.

He looked out the window.

"Slow day," he said after a while.

"It is. Just the two of us."

"And your father."

"And my father," Apple said, nodding. "Yep."

"I'm enjoying your company," Brian said.

"And I'm enjoying yours, Brian McKenna. I'm glad you stopped in."

"Me too."

"Did you ever know someone who changed your life forever?" Apple said.

Brian looked down into his glass. Smiled.

The door opened.

Rocky

"Put it under your shirt," Frank Dove whispered. "Do it *now*."

Jeff Bloom shook his head. "He's *watching*."

"No, he's not," Frank Dove whispered. "Just do it."

Jeff Bloom held the can of red spray paint and pretended to read the label.

"Can I help you boys with something?" Mike Kramer said from behind the counter. He had been watching the three of them.

"Uh, no. We're okay," Jeff Bloom said.

"You know, my hearing's real good," Mike Kramer said. "Your jerky friend there wants you to stuff that can of paint under your shirt and walk out without paying me. You do that, kid, and I'm gonna come around this counter and stuff that can of paint up your keister."

The three boys didn't move.

"And sideways," Mike Kramer said. "Put it back on the shelf and get the hell out of my store."

They did, and fast.

"So what are we supposed to do now?" Frank Dove said.

"I guess we'll have to pay for it," Paul Thanatos said. "We'll chip in."

167

"Why should *I* have to pay?" Jeff Bloom said. "And I ain't going back in there to buy it. That guy is nuts."

"You'll pay because we're all in this together," Paul Thanatos said. "Kepler threatened all *three* of us. She said you'd be the one driving the car, Jeff, and you were going to get us all killed when I'm just eighteen. *Me!* Maybe you should pay for the paint *yourself.* You're gonna be the driver."

"I ain't paying for all of it," Jeff Bloom said. "And I ain't dying on no Southern State Parkway when I'm eighteen."

"Well, that's what she said," Paul Thanatos said.

"Okay, we'll go chipsies," Jeff Bloom said. "Three ways. Let's just stop talking about it and do it. C'mon, let's go."

"Where we gonna go?" Frank Dove said.

"Kramers ain't the only hardware store in town," Jeff Bloom said. "I know another one, but it's a ride from here."

"How far?" Paul Thanatos said.

"About a half-hour," Jeff Bloom said.

"Okay," Paul Thanatos said. "Fewer witnesses. Let's get going." They climbed on their bikes.

Hannah sat in the dark, looking at the stars. Her parents were asleep.

A movement caught her eye.

Cat?

No.

Too big for a cat.

There. Again.

It was moving erratically.

"It's a raccoon," Hannah whispered to herself. She smiled and thought of the Rocky Raccoon song from the Beatles White Album, which had come out the previous year.

"Now somewhere in the Black Mountain Hills of Dakota there lived a young boy named Rocky Raccoon," she sang. "And one day his woman ran off with another guy."

The raccoon crawled into the storm drain across the street.

"Hit young Rocky in the eye," she crooned. "Rocky didn't like that. He said, I'm gonna get that boy."

Hannah smiled. "Goodbye, Rocky. Sweet dreams in your storm drain. I hope you get better soon."

She went back to looking at the stars.

"I come from you," she whispered to a particularly bright one. "You're mine and I'm yours. Forever."

"We should get black paint, not red," Paul Thanatos said earlier that day when they got to Cline Hardware.

"Red is more noticeable," Jeff Bloom said.

"But red was the color of their flag, not the color of the swastika," Paul Thanatos said. "The swastika was black. Look it up in the encyclopedia like I did."

"I ain't got no encyclopedia," Jeff Bloom said.

"He's right," Frank Dove said. "I seen the pictures. We're not going to paint the whole flag, just the swastika. It should be black. Paul's right."

"I always am," Paul Thanatos said.

"Okay," Jeff Bloom said. "Have it your way."

"It ain't *my* way," Paul Thanatos said. "It's the *right* way."

"Yeah, whatever. Let's just get it," Jeff Bloom said.

"And you're sure you're okay with this?" Paul Thanatos said.

"With what? The swastika?" Jeff Bloom said.

"Yeah."

"Why wouldn't I be?"

169

"Ain't you a Jew?"

"No."

"I thought you were," Paul Thanatos said. "Ain't Bloom a Jew name?"

"My parents are Jewish. I ain't," Jeff Bloom said.

"Then what are you?" Paul Thanatos said.

"I ain't nothing."

"Okay then," Paul Thanatos said. "Let's do it."

They left their bikes around the corner against a neighbor's privet hedge. They were wearing jeans, black sweatshirts with hoods and they were bent over, moving slowly, trying to blend into the shadows. Hannah watched them from her bedroom window, amused. They looked like crabs on a beach.

It's a warm night, she thought. They must be sweaty.

She turned toward the storm drain and went very still. Her lips moved, as if in prayer.

She saw its head between the grate. Its eyes reflected the light from the streetlamp a block away. They looked crazed.

Jeff Bloom had shaken the can of black spray paint before they left for Hannah's house, but he thought he should shake it again now, just in case. He did and it clicked like a tap dancer.

"Don't do that," Paul Thanatos hissed and stopped. They were in the middle of the road.

"I want to make sure it's mixed good," Jeff Bloom whispered.

"Stop it!"

He did.

"Sidewalk or driveway?" Frank Dove whispered.

Jeff Bloom pointed to the car, smiled and nodded, looking for approval.

Paul Thanatos shook his head. "We can get in too much trouble for that if someone comes out," he whispered. "Cars are off-limits. Do the sidewalk. Do it over there." He pointed. "Where it's dark. There."

Jeff Bloom snapped the cap off the can.

Hannah shifted her gaze from the storm drain to the three boys.

Jeff Bloom started by painting a large X on the sidewalk. He giggled.

"How's *that* for a start? The astronauts will be able to see this one from space. Did I get both lines the same length? They look pretty straight, don't they?"

"Finish it," Paul Thanatos hissed. "Put the little arms on it. You know how it goes, don't you?" Jeff Bloom nodded. "It's gotta look like a real swastika. Hurry up. Don't stand there admiring your work. We gotta get out of here. *Do it.*" He looked down the block.

The rabid raccoon bit deeply into Jeff Bloom's right calf as he lowered the can toward the end of one of the lines. Jeff Bloom's eyes went wide and he shrieked. Paul Thanatos and Frank Dove looked, jumped back, and then ran, which was something Jeff Bloom couldn't do just then.

Lights came on in several houses, including the Kepler house, but not in Hannah's room. Hannah sat still in the dark and watched it all.

Tiny smile.

She stared at the raccoon and went even stiller. Her lips moved silently. The raccoon released Jeff Bloom's calf. It hobbled back to the storm drain, and crawled in. Hannah wondered how such a large animal could fit thought such a tight opening.

"You're like a cat," she whispered.

She felt the raccoon nod yes.

Jeff Bloom was on the ground, crying. His jeans were bloody. His paint can rolled into the road.

"Thank you, Rocky," Hannah whispered.

With the raccoon gone, Paul Thanatos and Frank Dove hurried back to Jeff Bloom and helped him up. They moved as quickly as they could. Doors were opening and adults were coming out. The three boys got on their bikes and rode.

"You guys left me," Jeff Bloom said three blocks later.

"What were we supposed to do?" Paul Thanatos said. "You expect us to stand there and get bit, too?"

"You *left* me!"

"We gotta get him to a doctor," Frank Dove said.

"I ain't going to no doctor," Jeff Bloom said. "They ask too many questions at the doctor. I'll just wash it with soap and water when I get home. You guys shouldn't have left me. That was wrong. We're supposed to be a team. We're supposed to be friends."

"We came back, didn't we?" Paul Thanatos said.

"Yeah, but you left the paint there. I paid for some of that paint."

"You're worried about the paint?" Paul Thanatos said.

"I gotta get this bite washed out," Jeff Bloom cried as he peddled. "It hurts so bad."

"You sure you don't want a doc?" Frank Dove said. "That raccoon could have rabies."

"Raccoons don't get rabies," Jeff Bloom said. "Only dogs get rabies. Everybody knows that."

"You sure?" Frank Dove said.

"Yeah, I'm sure," Jeff Bloom said. "I just gotta wash it out good with soap and water. I'll be okay."

Paul Thanatos was riding fifty feet ahead of them, looking over his shoulder and motioning for them to hurry up, but Jeff Bloom couldn't peddle that fast. Frank Dove pedaled up to Paul Thanatos. "You should slow down," he said. He can't go that fast."

"Tough," Paul Thanatos said. "He shouldn't have gotten bit."

"Do you know if raccoons can't have rabies?" Frank Dove said. "That's what Jeff said. That they *can't*. You heard him."

"He's wrong. They *can* have rabies," Paul Thanatos said, looking straight ahead.

"Jeff doesn't believe it."

"Then Jeff's gonna die," Paul Thanatos said.

"What are we gonna do?" Frank Dove said. "He won't listen to me."

Paul Thanatos pedaled faster.

"Slow down. I said what are we gonna do?"

"Listen," Paul Thanatos said, slowing. "If he dies, then that means the Kepler bitch was wrong with her prediction. It also means me and you are in the clear. Jeff can't kill us in his car on the Southern State Parkway when we're eighteen if he's dead from rabies now. Just keep your mouth shut and we'll see how this goes. He made up his mind about the raccoon bite. No doctor. No hospital. That's what he said, right? That's what he wants, right? Well, it's his call, so now we just wait and let nature take its course. We were never there at the bitch's house.

173

Just keep saying that, Frank. Jeff never finished the swastika. It's just a big X on the sidewalk. Like X marks the spot where we never were. Okay? They'll probably wash it off in the morning and that will be that. It never happened. Okay?"

Frank Dove said nothing.

"Okay?" Paul Thanatos snarled.

"Yeah, yeah, okay. We'll do it *your* way."

"*Our* way. You're in this as deep as I am, Frank. Don't you *ever* forget that," Paul Thanatos said. "Don't try to screw me by talking about this to anyone."

"I won't, Paul. Relax, okay?"

"Don't you tell me to relax. You just do as you're told."

Frank Dove dropped back to ride with Jeff Bloom, who would be dead eight weeks later.

Delaney's
2018

"You forget something?" Apple said. Her father had come through the door as quickly as he could, considering his arthritis. He stopped 10 feet behind Brian's stool, his cane tapping the floor in front of him.

He stared at Brian and didn't answer Apple. Tapped. Tapped.

"You forget something?" Apple repeated, going stiff.

He didn't answer.

Tap.

Tap.

Brian turned on his stool to face him. He smiled. "Welcome back," he said.

"Why are you smiling?" Apple's father said.

"Excuse me?" Brian said.

"I said why are you *smiling*?" He lifted the cane and pointed it at Brian. "You're not my friend. Why are you *smiling*?"

"I'm smiling because it's a *beautiful* day," Brian said, still smiling.

"I don't think it's so beautiful," Apple's father said. "What's so beautiful about it? It looks like it's going to *rain*."

"If it's going to rain, that will be good for the flowers and the grass," Brian said. "We need rain. It's been dry lately."

"It's *not* a nice day," Apple's father said. "I just said that. What part of that don't you understand. Are you stupid?"

"Don't," Apple said.

Her father ignored her.

"Okay, then, we'll have it your way," Brian said. "It's *not* a nice day, but let's hope the day gets better." Brian started to turn back toward Apple.

"How's the day supposed to get *better*?" Apple's father said. "You gonna die in the next few minutes? *That* would sure make it better."

"Stop!" Apple said.

Brian turned toward him again but said nothing.

"I asked you a *question,* mister. You gonna die in the next few minutes?"

"I suppose only God knows the answer to that question," Brian said.

"There is no God," Apple's father said.

"Okay, then I suppose God *doesn't* know the answer. After all, there *is* no God. We'll have it your way. That's fine by me."

"*What's* fine by you?," Apple's father said. "That you don't believe in God?"

"Sure," Brian said. "If that's what you want."

"I was making a joke. What are you, one of those atheists who doesn't believe in anything? What sort of an unbelieving punk *are* you?"

Brian said nothing.

"You're a small-minded *punk* who doesn't know *what* you think, aren't you?"

Brian smiled at that.

"You smile at me? You *smile*. Like a *clown*. Are you a *clown*?"

Brian kept smiling.

"You don't smile at a man unless that man is your friend. I'm not your *friend*, mister."

Brian said nothing.

"Don't start in here," Apple said. "I need this job. I told you that. You said you had changed. I knew you were lying."

Her father ignored her.

"You hear what I'm saying to you, mister?" he said to Brian.

Brian said nothing.

"Don't!" Apple shouted. She reached for her phone. "I'll call them. You *know* I will. They'll be here in minutes. You know how close the precinct house is. They'll lock you up. Don't make me do this."

"You disrespected me when I was leaving before," Apple's father said to Brian. "You think I need the door opened for me? You think I'm *weak?* I'm probably younger than you are, you bastard. Who the hell do you think you are treating *me* with disrespect?"

Brian said nothing.

Apple's father pointed his cane at Brian like a sword. "I'll bust you up if you ever try that again. You hear me? And why are you in here in the first place? You come in here to prey on the young girls?" He pointed the cane at his daughter. "She must be forty years younger than you. Why don't you find someone your own age? You a pedophile? You like to hang out at the elementary schools? You like to stare at the little girls?"

Brian said nothing.

Apple started to dial "You're done," she said.

"You finish that beer and get out. You hear me? That's your *last*. If I see you in here again there's going to be trouble."

"Get out of here!" Apple screamed. *"Now!"*

He pointed his cane at Brian again, hobbled to the door, and left.

"I'm so sorry," Apple said.

"Don't be," Brian said. "He is who he is, and I was in the wrong place at the right time."

"You're in the *right* place, and at the *right* time," Apple said. She reached over and squeezed his hand.

"I'll leave in a minute. One more sip," Brian said, lifting his glass. "I don't want to bring you anymore trouble than I already have."

"No," Apple said. "No!" She drew a fresh pint and set it on a new coaster. She knocked the bar twice with her knuckles. "On me. It's *my* turn to buy back," she said. "You're staying."

Brian said nothing.

"He won't be back in here today," she said. "I know him."

"You sure?" Brian said.

"Yes, and you never answered my question."

"What question?"

"Did you ever know someone who changed your life forever?"

Brian looked into his pint.

Apple waited.

He nodded. "Yes."

Richie
6:00 A.M.

Richie was stretched across the back seat of the Mustang. He woke on the third tap.

Brian smiled and held up the bottle of Tropicana orange juice. Hannah was standing beside him.

"Good morning," Richie said, climbing out of the car. He stretched.

"Richie, this is Hannah. She's helping me do the milk."

Richie held out his hand. Hannah looked at it for a moment and then took it. Her hand was as big as his.

"It's nice to meet you, Hannah," Richie said.

"Nice to meet you," Hannah said.

Richie, at five-foot six, was looking up at both of them.

"Do your parents know you're doing the milk, Hannah?"

"No."

"Why not?" Richie said.

"They haven't asked me."

"They don't know you're out all night?" Richie said.

"No."

"Why not?"

"Because they're sleeping, Richie," Hannah said.

"Shouldn't they be watching you?"

"Watching me do what?" Hannah said.

"Just watching you. You're underage," Richie said.

"Under what age?"

"I guess sixteen?" Richie said. "You're fifteen, right? You're a child."

"No, I'm not a child, Richie," Hannah said. "Children don't do the milk."

"They don't," Brian said, shaking his head. "You have to be a grown-up to do the milk, even if you're a helper. Hannah is my helper. You have to be able to carry everything and find the milk boxes. Hannah is very good at everything, just like I am. She's strong, and she's fast, and even stays home alone sometimes."

"But there must be an age when you can't be left alone at home," Richie said.

"It's up to the parents," Hannah said. "That's the law. I read about it in the library. And my parents don't want me to be with them. They know I'm home by myself. They give me money. I walk to the grocery store. I lock the doors. I don't light candles. I don't smoke. I've been home alone often. I'm used to it. My parents like to travel without me. My mother says they're under a lot of stress, and the places they visit are too nice for me."

Richie stared at Hannah, and then at Brian.

"I can also get married if I want to get married, and without their permission. Did you know that, Richie?"

"At fifteen?" Richie said.

"No, at *fourteen*. It's the law in New York State. If you go to the library you can see for yourself. I can show you."

"Do you want to get married, Hannah?"

"No, not today. I'm reading a book today."

Richie looked at Brian, who shrugged.

"Is there anything else I can help you understand, Richie?" Hannah said.

Richie said nothing.

"Isn't the juice beautiful?" Hannah said, pointing at the bottle and smiling.

Richie looked at the bottle and nodded. He twisted the cap and took a sip. "Yes, it is," he said. "Thank you."

"It's the gift of the trees," Hannah said. "When you drink their juice, you should thank them. You're getting some of their energy with each sip. You're also getting energy from the ice that cools the juice. Water has a lot of energy, even when it's frozen, especially when it's frozen. The energy is concentrated when the water is frozen."

Richie stared at her. He took another sip.

Hannah smiled.

Richie held out the bottle. Hannah took it from him, smiled and drank deeply.

"It's so good," Hannah said, giggling like a little girl. Some of the juice was on her chin. She laughed and wiped it with the back of her hand.

Richie watched her.

"Thank you for sharing with me, Richie," Hannah said. "And for caring about me. Would you like another bottle of juice? Or maybe a bottle of milk? Milk is a gift from the mothers. You can have it for your journey, or for Fiona. She's hungry."

Richie stared at Hannah.

"Richie?" Brian said after a moment.

"Um. Oh, no. Thank you, Hannah," Richie said.

"You're welcome," she said. "We have to go now, Richie. Popeye needs to take me home so I can read my book. And then he has to bring the empties back to the plant so they can wash them and fill them up again with milk for tomorrow's route. Then he'll go home to his mother."

"Popeye?" Richie said.

"Yes," Hannah said, nodding toward Brian. "Popeye."

Richie looked at Brian.

"You should take more juice from us for your journey," Hannah said.

"My journey," Richie said.

"Yes."

"It's not far. It's just a few miles," Richie said, rubbing his eyes.

"You should take more juice," Hannah said. "The trees' energy will help you."

"It's not far. Really."

Hannah walked back to the truck and returned with two quarts of orange juice, very cold from the ice. She handed them to Richie. "Here," she said. "Please take them. They will help you on your journey. Do you want milk? For Fiona?"

Richie took the two bottles of juice. "I don't need milk," he said.

Hannah smiled, nodded, and turned. She walked back to the Chevy and got in.

Richie stared at her. She was looking at Fiona, the calico house cat, who was sitting on The Landing Strip's wide windowsill, staring back at her. Hannah's lips were moving, showing her small, white teeth. Who is she talking to? Richie wondered.

"Thanks, Richie," Brian said. "I'm glad you got to meet Hannah."

"Should I call you Popeye now?" Richie said.

"Call me Brian."

"What are you *doing* with this girl? Who *is* she?"

"I told you, Richie. She's one of the customers. She's helping me do the milk. Like I used to help Ole Olson do the milk. But I don't back into the streets like Ole used to do to put most of the deliveries on my side of the truck. Hannah and I share the stops, fair and square. We work fast."

"Are you paying her money?"

"I offered to pay her, but she said no. She just wants to be with the milk and with the ice. And I guess with me too. We listen to Long John Nebel on the radio."

"Are you doing anything else with her, Brian?"

"No. I told you that. I promise."

"Why did she give me this juice?" Richie said, holding out the two quart bottles. "What is this business about my *journey*? I'm just going to drive home."

"I don't know, Richie. I wish I did."

Richie looked at Hannah sitting in the truck. Her eyes were closed. She was smiling.

"I have to go, Richie. So long." Brian walked to the Chevy.

"Richie is going away," Hannah said.

"How do you know?" Brian said.

"Fiona told me."

Brian drove. He said nothing.

He never saw Richie again.

Fiona

"We have to wait until it's six o'clock before we can wake him up," Brian said to Hannah on that last day. They were parked a car-length behind the Mustang.

"Why, Popeye?" Hannah said.

"We just do. I always tap him awake at six o'clock. He doesn't get much sleep to begin with, and I don't want to wake him ten minutes early."

"Okay," Hannah said.

They sat and watched the car, gleaming in the dawn.

"I love that car," Brian said.

"Whose cat is that?" Hannah said. She was looking at The Landing Strip's wide front window. The calico cat was sitting up, staring at them.

"That's Fiona. She's not really anybody's cat. Or I guess she's *everybody's* cat. She lives in the bar. She's a bar cat. I don't know how long she's lived there. I think she catches mice to earn her keep."

Hannah nodded, and went very still.

"*Milk,*" Fiona said in Hannah's mind.

"Are you hungry, dear Fiona?" Hannah said silently.

"Yes."

"Is someone there to feed you?" Hannah said.

"Man," Fiona said.

"Is he a good man, Fiona?"

"Yes."

"Then he will feed you when it is time," Hannah said.

"Going away," Fiona said.

"Who?"

"Man."

"Why?"

"Danger."

"Where will he go?"

"Far," Fiona said.

"Why does he have to go?"

"Men coming."

"How do you know this?" Hannah said.

"I see. I see. I see. I see. I see. I see." Fiona was turning in circles on the windowsill.

"Is it the man in the car?" Hannah said.

"Yes. Yes. Yes. Yes. Yes."

"Will he be safe if he leaves today?" Hannah said.

"Milk," Fiona said.

"Are you in danger?" Hannah said.

Fiona shivered.

"Popeye will come for you and keep you safe," Hannah said. "Soon."

Fiona jumped off the wide windowsill and was gone.

"Okay," Brian said. "It's six o'clock now. We can wake him up."

They got out of the Chevy. Hannah pulled Richie's orange juice from the ice. She handed it to Brian and took his other hand. They walked toward the Mustang.

The Landing Strip

Charlie Payne was tending bar. Brian had never seen him do that before. It had always been Richie. Charlie Payne showed up now and then to take care of some things in his office. He'd stop at the bar when he was done, and maybe have a Coke and listen to the conversation for a while. He really didn't join in the conversation. He just listened. Everyone knew he was the owner, but Brian had never spoken to him because Charlie had never asked Brian any questions.

Brian sat on the stool at the right end of the semicircle. It was his usual spot, the closest thing you could get to having a seat in the back row when you were dealing with a semicircle. The guys who did the most talking sat in the center of the semicircle. Those were the power stools.

Charlie flipped a cardboard Schaefer coaster onto the bar in front of Brian.

"How you doin', kid?" he said.

"I'm good. Where's Richie?"

"Ain't here. What are you havin'?"

"Is he okay?"

"What is this? Twenty questions?" Charlie said. "I told you he ain't here."

"I'm worried about him," Brian said.

"You'd better start worrying about yourself if you keep asking about things that are none of your business, kid."

Brian said nothing.

"What are you *havin'*?"

"Schaefer?"

"The one beer to have when you're having more than one," Charlie said. "You having more than one, kid?" Charlie drew the shortie and set it on the coaster.

"I usually have three," Brian said.

"A big spender," Charlie said. "I ain't gettin' rich on you, kid."

Brian said nothing.

Charlie stood there waiting.

"Twenty cents," he said.

"Oh," Brian fumbled for a dollar bill and placed it next to the coaster. "Sorry," he said.

"I ain't your banker, kid. Pay as you go." Charlie picked up the dollar, made change, and set it down in front of Brian. He turned and looked around for empty glasses.

"You see those murders?" Jake said to no one in particular.

"Yeah, ain't that something?" Ed said.

"She was a beautiful woman," Jake said.

"And about to have a baby, I hear," Ed said. "What sort of animal can kill a beautiful woman like that, and her baby?"

"And there were others," Tom said.

"What was her name?" Bill said.

"Sharon Tate," Ed said. "She was in that movie that was a big hit a couple of years ago. Valley of the Dolls."

"That was a dirty moving, wasn't it?" Jake said. "I think she was married to that guy Polanski. The director. He wasn't there. Lucky thing for him."

"I don't know how you can call that guy lucky," Tom said.

"Well, I mean he was lucky that he wasn't there to get killed," Jake said.

"Maybe he could have defended her," Ed said.

"Maybe. Maybe not," Jake said. "Who knows."

"What kind of animal does that?" Ed said.

None of the drinkers mentioned Richie not being there. Brian wondered whether he should ask them if they knew where he was, but then he thought about how Charlie the owner had reacted when he had asked him about Richie.

"On a happier note, gents," Jake said, raising his glass. "Yesterday was the twenty-fourth anniversary of the day we dropped the big one on Nagasaki. I wish we could do it all over again and roast some more of them Japs."

Everyone but Brian toasted.

Jake looked hard at Brian.

"And did you hear about this other thing that's coming up? This big rock-and-roll show somewhere in the Catskills?" Ed said.

"Yeah," Jake said. "It's a hippie thing, right? No big deal. I mean it's not like Elvis is gonna be there."

"I hear it's gonna be pretty big, though," Ed said. "I hear they may get a few thousand people to that thing. What are the calling that thing? Stock or stick, or something like that, isn't it?"

"Woodstock," Tom said.

Brian hadn't heard about the murders in California, or about Woodstock. He had heard about Nagasaki. His father had talked about that a lot, but no more. He looked into his beer.

"You going to that thing, Brian?" Jake said from his power stool. "You're a hippie, right?" The men all turned toward Brian and laughed. "You been letting your hair grow, ain't you? You a hippie now, Brian? You leaving us regular hard-working men to be a hippie now? You going on welfare, Brian? This gonna be your summer of love? You gonna be screwing the hippie chicks?"

"I haven't had time to get a haircut," Brian said, touching his hair. "I will. I've just been busy doing the milk and taking care of my mother. She's been coughing a lot."

"I think he's turning hippie, guys," Jake said, looking around the semicircle. "I think he's gonna give up the beers and switch to pot. You gonna switch to pot, Brian? Let your hair grow down to your ass? I hear the hippie chicks like that. Tough to wipe your ass with all that hair in the way, but I hear they like that. Gonna have some shit in your hair, Brian?"

"No," Brian said.

"I think he's gonna switch to pot," Jake said. "What do you guys think?"

One by one, the guys turned on Brian, and Richie wasn't there to help him.

"He's a hippie!" Jake shouted, "He's gonna be burning his draft card before we know it. I can see it coming. You gonna burn your draft card, hippie boy? You gonna go down South and march with your colored friends?"

"No," Brian said.

"Oh, that's right," Jake said. "You got your easy out from the Draft Board, didn't you? Your mommy went down there and got it for you, didn't she? You don't have to fight for your country like the rest of us brave men did, do you? You got your out, didn't you?"

"Yes," Brian said.

"That right, kid?" Charlie Payne said, walking over to Brian. "You dodging the draft? That *right*?"

"No."

"Well, then why ain't you over there fighting the Commies?" Charlie Payne said. "I've been wondering about that all summer when I seen you in here. This is an American bar, you know. Only patriots drink in here."

"That's right," Jake said. "You tell him, Charlie."

"I'm exempt," Brian said. "I do the milk. My mother needs me to do the milk. I'm all that she has left."

Charlie Payne looked around the room. The men had gone quiet, waiting.

"Well, I'll tell you what, kid," Charlie Payne said. "I think it's time for you to get out of my bar and go home to your mommy and your milk. These here men are building war planes to fight the Commies. You don't deserve to be drinking with them. Get out of my bar."

Brian looked around the semicircle. Richie wasn't there to help him. No one was smiling.

Brian got off his stool. He left his change on the bar.

"Hey, wait a minute, draft dodger," Charlie Payne said, picking up the coins. "Take your filthy money with you. It's no good in here." He threw the coins at Brian. They hit him in his face and fell to the floor. The men all laughed. Brian didn't pick them up.

He shoved the door open and heard the men applaud. Fiona slipped out between his legs before the door closed.

Pathmark

The white envelope taped to the storm door had his name on it. Brian opened it and read the note.

Because of your bad behavior, you are no longer welcome in my home. From now on, you are to bring the route book with my money to the back of the house. Under the awning, you will see a red picnic cooler. You will place the route book with my money in the cooler and take the other route book with you. You are to do this every day and not ever knock on my door again. I do not want to see you in my home because of the way you behaved the other day. You should be ashamed of yourself, trying to take advantage of a widow the way you did.

She signed it with her full name: Mrs. Mae Alice Olson.

Brian thought about how he had helped her stand up when she had reached for him and fallen under the table. Was that bad behavior? Should he have left her under the table? As soon as she was up, she had tried to grab him again. Was that his fault?

Brian folded the note and put it in his back pocket. He walked to the backyard and exchanged the route books. On his way back to the truck, he saw a curtain move.

He got into the truck and put the route book on the bench seat. He realized she hadn't written anything about how he would be paid in the future. Ole Olson had always paid him in cash, and every day. Mae had done the same until last week, until the day she had fallen drunk under the table. She owed him for last week. For the whole thing. His mother needed that money.

He sat in the truck and thought about what to do. The curtain moved again.

He got out of the truck and walked back into the yard. She was taking the route book out of the cooler. She screamed. He ran.

Before he went to her house the next morning, Brian opened some of the envelopes and took out the cash that she owned him. He wrote a note explaining what he had done and put the route book back into the cooler.

The following day, as he did the route, he noticed that some of the customers had decided to cancel their deliveries. Mae Olson had placed notes on these pages, but she had not made any changes to the directions-to-the-next-house codes. Brian corrected the book as he went along. He knew the route by heart now, but he was thinking about the next person who may have this job. He wondered how long he would be allowed to do it.

The next day, several more people dropped their deliveries. Brian mentioned this to his mother when he got home.

"I think it's the new Pathmark," Grace McKenna said.

"What do you mean?" Brian said.

"Here. Look," she said, opening *Newsday* to the full-page Pathmark ad.

"Where did you get the paper?" Brian said.

"Annie from next door brought it over," Grace McKenna said.

The ad featured a lot of things, but in the center was a waxed-cardboard container of milk and the printed question, "Why pay more?" The quart of milk in the ad costs 25 cents. Olson's Dairy was charging 35 cents for the same milk. Sure, it was in a glass bottle, but still. That's a big difference. Beer costs 20 cents. For every two quarts of milk, you have enough savings to buy a beer.

How many more people will quit?

"Mrs. Olson charges us fifty cents a quart now," his mother said. "She's been raising the price since Mr. Olson passed. I didn't want to tell you."

"We should go to Pathmark for our milk from now on," Brian said.

"Yes," his mother said.

Another note taped to the route book.

We are losing these customers because of the poor way you're doing your job!!! If you don't do a better job I will replace you with someone else!!! This is fair warning!!!

She didn't sign the note.

Sweet Wine

"I don't like the way we just let Jeff die," Frank Dove said. "I really think we should have done something."

"Done something?" Paul Thanatos said. "Like what? He didn't want us to do something. It was his choice not to go to the doctor."

"Yeah, I know that. But still."

"What do you mean, but *still*?" Paul Thanatos said.

"I think we should say something to somebody. I feel lousy about this whole thing. We were just fooling around, painting that swastika, even though Jeff never got it done. And it was all your idea to begin with."

"I recall we came up with the idea together, Frank," Paul Thanatos said, stepping closer to Frank Dove. "The *three* of us. And are you losing your mind? You want both of us to wind up in jail?"

"How we gonna wind up in jail?" Frank Dove said. "We didn't make that raccoon bite him. We were just there when it happened."

"But we were there breaking the law," Paul Thanatos said. "Don't you get it? If we weren't there, he never would have gotten bit, and that's what the judge will look at. You want to go to juvenile detention? You know what they do to you in juvenile detention?"

"I just feel so bad, Paul. He was our friend. We left him there."

"No, we didn't leave him there. We went back for him when we could," Paul Thanatos said. "We helped him get away."

"Yeah, but then you said let nature take its course, and if he dies we'll be off the hook for what the Kepler bitch said to you about dying on the Southern State Parkway."

"You trying to put this whole thing on me, Frank? You better not be. You're in this as much as I am. Nothing we do can bring Jeff back. He died because he didn't want to go to the doctor. We can't change that. We just gotta forget about it and get on with our lives."

"Aww, I don't know, Paul. I'm not sure I can do that."

"Okay, so how about this. Let's think on it overnight. Tomorrow's Saturday. Maybe we'll go for a bike ride. Somewhere we can talk more. Somewhere quiet. I'll get us some cigarettes. We can smoke together and talk. That's a good way to think. Smoking will help us think, okay?"

"Where you gonna get cigarettes?"

"My mother's got a carton she just bought. I'll take a pack. She won't miss it. I'll take it from the back end of the carton. By the time she smokes her way to that point in the carton she'll think she was the one that smoked them all. She smokes like a chimney."

"Okay." Frank Dove said. "I gotta mow the lawn in the morning. I can meet you at eleven."

"Okay. We'll ride the bikeway and smoke in the woods by the pond. And I'll bring some drinks and snacks for us."

"Okay," Frank Dove said.

"Yeah, we'll talk. Just you and me. We'll talk and smoke."

"Okay," Frank Dove said.

Paul Thanatos knew that his father always kept a few gallons of Prestone antifreeze in his garage. His father bought it at the end of each winter when it went on sale at the auto-parts store. The yellow containers always caught Paul Thanatos' eye when he was taking out the trash.

Paul had been in the Boy Scouts when he was 11, but he didn't like the way the scoutmaster tried to tell him what to do. His old uniform was balled-up on the floor of his closet, but he still used the knapsack and the aluminum canteen his parents had gotten him for the one Boy Scout jamboree he had gone to. They were both good for long bike rides.

He had heard some things about Prestone from the older boys at school. The boys he wanted to be like. The tough boys. They shared certain things with him. Secrets. He carried the canteen out to the garage and filled it with the Prestone. His father wouldn't miss it. He tightened the cap and carried it into the kitchen.

"I'm going to put this in the freezer," he told his mother.

"But it will freeze," she said, thinking it was water and not antifreeze.

"I know, but that's what I want it to do. I'm going to take a long bike ride tomorrow and if it's frozen it will stay colder longer on the ride." Paul knew the Prestone wouldn't freeze but he didn't want his mother opening it before he left to meet Frank Dove.

"Where are you going to go?" his mother said.

"I don't know. Just around. The weather's supposed to be nice. I like riding my bike when it's nice out."

"I know you do. You going with anyone?"

"Nah, just by myself."

"Okay." she said and lit another cigarette. "Be careful."

"I sure will," he said.

They rode the bikeway that runs parallel to Bethpage Parkway to the point where Bethpage Parkway ends and connects to the Southern State Parkway, the road on which Hannah said they would all die when Paul Thanatos was 18. He smiled at that, knowing that it wasn't going to happen now. Jeff Bloom was dead.

There's a small pond with no name at that point of the bikeway, and the two boys stopped to look at the ducks and the big turtles.

"Pond's got a lot of scum on it this year," Frank Dove said.

Paul Thanatos nodded. "Let's ride around to the other side," he said. "We can smoke in the woods over there. No one ever goes over that way."

"That's good," Frank Dove said. "If my mother ever catches me smoking I'm in big trouble."

"Yeah, me, too," Paul Thanatos said. "No one will see us back there, and I brought some of my mother's Sen-Sen for our breath when we're done."

"That's good. Did you remember to bring the matches?"

"Yeah."

"Bring any snacks?"

"I got pretzels and something special."

"What?"

"Sweet wine," Paul Thanatos said, holding up his Boy Scout canteen. "You'll like it."

"Is it real sweet?"

"It's sweet like Kool-Aid," Paul Thanatos said. "You're gonna love it. It gets you high as a kite."

"You're the best, Paul! You really know how to throw a party."

"Well, I want you to be happy, Frank. That way, maybe you'll stop talking about calling somebody and telling them about what we did."

"Yeah, I been thinking that maybe you're right, Paul. Maybe we should just keep it to ourselves. We can't bring Jeff back."

"Now you're talking smart," Paul Thanatos said.

They went far enough back into the woods so that no one could see them. They leaned their bikes against a scrub pine tree and Paul took two Kent cigarettes out of the pack.

"I wish your mom smoked Marlboros instead of Kents," Frank Dove said. "Kents are girlie cigarettes."

"Beggars can't be choosers," Paul Thanatos said.

He lit his cigarette and held the match out for Frank Dove, who inhaled and coughed.

"You okay?" Paul Thanatos said.

"Yeah, I'm okay." He coughed again. "Just not used to it."

"Take it slow. We're in no rush," Paul Thanatos said.

Frank Dove tried to blow a smoke ring but it didn't work for him.

"You suck at that," Paul Thanatos said.

"You try it," Frank Dove said.

Paul Thanatos did, and had the same result as Frank Dove.

"I guess we both suck at it," Frank Dove said.

"Takes practice," Paul Thanatos said. "We need to smoke more often."

They finished their cigarettes and crushed out the butts on a rock.

"Make sure it's out," Frank Dove said. "We don't want to start a fire back here."

"It's out," Paul Thanatos said.

"How much pretzels did you bring?"

201

"I got a whole box," Paul Thanatos said, reaching into his Boy Scout knapsack.

"Mister Salty!" Frank Dove said. "Those are the best! Give 'em here." Frank Dove reached for them.

"Have as much as you want," Paul Thanatos said.

"Thanks."

"They're good, ain't they?"

"So good," Frank Dove said.

"You thirsty?

"I am. Let me try some of that sweet wine you brought. I ain't never had any of that before."

Paul smiled and reached for the canteen. He handed it to Frank Dove.

"It's ice cold," Frank Dove said.

"It tastes best that way," Paul Thanatos said.

"Yeah?"

"Yeah. Take a big drink. It'll get you high as a kite. There's plenty there. Take as much as you want."

"You sure?"

"Positive," Paul Thanatos said. "Bottoms up!"

Frank Dove unscrewed the cap and took a small sip. "It's real sweet," he said.

"Have more. It will get you high."

"Okay." Frank Dove drank deeply.

"That's the way to do it," Paul Thanatos said. "Take more."

"What about you?"

"There's plenty. I don't want to share your spit. I'll go when you're done."

"Okay," Frank Dove said, drinking more.

Paul Thanatos sat and watched.

Waited.

"Gimme another one of those smokes," Frank Dove said. Paul Thanatos was happy to oblige.

"My heart's beating real fast," Frank Dove said.

"That's the cigarettes. Don't worry about it," Paul Thanatos said.

Frank Dove moved his hand to his throat. His breathing was labored.

"I don't feel so good," he said.

"Get up and walk around a bit," Paul Thanatos said, helping him up. Frank Dove was unsteady on his feet. Paul Thanatos sat down again.

"I feel sick to my stomach," Frank Dove said.

"Walk it off," Paul Thanatos said. "It's the pretzels. Mr. Salty's got a lot of salt. Go walk it off."

Frank Dove turned, took three shaky steps, and fell forward. His throat hit the branch of a fallen tree, fracturing his larynx. He gagged. Gagged. His eyes went wide. He grabbed his throat with both hands. His face was turning blue. Paul Thanatos sat and watched him.

When Frank Dove stopped moving, Paul Thanatos policed the area, picking up the crushed butts. He put the pretzels and the canteen back in his knapsack. He looked around one more time. Then he got on his bike and rode home. He dumped the canteen in a storm drain a mile away from the pond.

Paul Thanatos smiled, knowing it was now impossible for him to be in a car with either Jeff Bloom or Frank Dove when he was 18 years old.

The Kepler bitch was just making it all up. He was sure of that now. He was in the clear. Finally, in the clear.

And maybe someday, he'd go see her too.

Delaney's
2018

"So who changed your life forever?" Apple said.

Brian looked up from his pint.

"I'd have to say Richie," Brian said.

"How so?"

"He taught me that I have to stand up for myself."

"How did he do that?"

"By disappearing and leaving me on my own."

Apple nodded. Waited.

"I never realized that he was defending me in here. I mean when it was The Landing Strip."

"Defending you against what?"

"Meanness," Brian said. "There were people who drank in here who seemed nice, but there was always an edge to them. They liked to poke at you, and if you got upset they'd say you couldn't take a joke."

"I know just what you mean," Apple said.

"Richie watched for when they'd start that with me. I was too young to understand what it was all about. I was enthralled by those guys. They were older than me. They built airplanes. They had families. They had been to war. I looked up to them. My brother drank with them. I thought I could be like my brother, but I could never be as good as he was at anything."

"What would Richie do when the men got like that?" Apple said.

"It depended on the guy. I realize that now when I think about it. I didn't really understand it then. Sometimes, he'd lean in and whisper something to a guy and that guy would suddenly get friendly again. Other times, he'd just look at the guy from way over there. He had a look that could freeze you in place. He wasn't a big guy but they respected him. And he was running the race book, so he was also holding all their money. I sometimes wonder if that had anything to do with it, or if he was connected with dangerous people. I don't know."

"Were some of the guys in debt to Richie?" Apple said.

"Maybe. I don't know."

"He was good to you."

"He was. He kept me safe. So did Ole Olson, the milkman. They kept me safe. When they were gone, I had to figure out how to keep myself safe. That took a while. Years."

"What makes people do those mean things?" Apple said. "My father takes that to the extreme. I've never understood why."

"I don't know," Brian said. "Maybe it's the booze talking. I wanted so bad to be a part of that crowd because my brother was a part of it. Or at least I thought he was. Maybe I got that wrong, too. Maybe he had as tough a time as I did in here. I'll never know. It bothers me that I'll never know."

"What happened at the end?" Apple said, and Brian told her about that last night and how they had all turned on him.

"I've seen that happen in other bars," Apple said.

"It hurt," Brian said.

"I know. My mother tried to protect me from my father, but she couldn't. I knew she was trying, though, and that mattered to me. She tried."

"I thought I was one of the guys. I had no idea it would all turn around as soon as Richie left. I mean that very same day."

"And that's what changed your life," Apple said. "It made you a better person. Be grateful for that."

"It did make me a better person. And I am grateful for it. But I sort of cratered after that day."

"What do you mean?" Apple said.

"I avoided people. I had plenty of time to think, and that got a little dangerous."

"Thinking," Apple said.

"Yes. I didn't know myself back then. I drank more than I should have, but all by myself, and at home. That wasn't good. My mother worried about me, and that troubled me. But she didn't last much longer. The cancer got to her, and then I was on my own. I was thinking too much, *feeling* too much."

"Did you have any friends?" Apple said.

"There was a girl. A few years younger than me. I think she was my friend."

"You think? You didn't know?"

"She was different. Like no one else I have ever known."

"What was her name?"

"Hannah."

"Did you love her?"

"No. She was my friend."

"Did she love you?"

"I don't know."

Apple waited.

The ice machine hummed.

"Was this a long time ago?" Apple said.

"Yes, a very long time ago. When I was doing the milk. I was eighteen."

"How old was Hannah?"

"Fifteen."

He turned and looked out the window.

"Do you think it was a good thing that Richie left for good?"

Brian turned back and smiled.

"I don't know," he said. "Nothing was ever the same after that, but I don't know if it was better or worse. It was just what it was."

"Life," Apple said.

Brian nodded.

"Yes," he said. "Life."

Apple

"It never took me that long to do *my* homework," Apple's father said. "Why does it take you so long?"

"I have to concentrate," Apple said.

"Why is it taking you so long?"

"Please let me concentrate."

"Are my questions bothering you?"

"I have to *concentrate*. This is difficult."

"People who are smart are able to do more than one thing at a time," her father said. "You can't seem to do that. Do you know what that means? Do you? It means that you're not so smart. It means that you're stupid."

"Dad, please."

"What? You think you're smart? You can't even do your homework and have a conversation with your father at the same time. That's not smart. That's stupid. Very, very stupid."

Apple said nothing.

"Your mother is the same way," he said. "I think you're both stupid. Both of you. You can't do more than one thing at a time. I can do many things at the same time. Do you know why? Do you? I can do many things at the same time because I am not stupid."

Apple said nothing.

"You have to agree with me," he said. "You are stupid. Agree with me."

She looked up at him.

"*Agree* with me," he said.

"Okay, I agree with you," Apple said.

"About *what*?"

"About what you just said."

"What did I just say?" he said.

"That Mom and I are stupid."

"Is that what you think I said. I never said that. What's wrong with you? Why would I say that you're stupid? Do *you* think you're stupid?"

"No, I don't, but you do," Apple said.

"How can you say that?"

"Dad, please leave me alone. I need to do my homework."

"You'd better find someone smart to marry," he said. "That's all I can say. Find someone smart, like your mother did. Stupid people should always marry smart people. Stupid people need smart people to tell them what to do."

Apple said nothing.

"It's true. You'd better marry someone smart. You'll never make it on your own. You're too stupid."

"I wish you would leave her alone," her mother said from the kitchen.

"Mind your business!" he shouted.

"Why are you always reading that Glamour magazine?" he said Apple. "You think you're glamorous? I don't think you're glamorous. You're not tall. The girls in the magazine are tall. They're glamorous. You're not."

"Please leave her alone," her mother said.

"You shut up. I'm talking to *her*," her father said.

"You think you look like those girls in that magazine? Do you?"

Apple said nothing.

"Well, you don't look like them. Just so you know. You *don't*. They're pretty. They're models. You're no model. You'll never be in a magazine. No one will ever want to marry you."

"Why are you *doing* this to me?" Apple cried.

"What? What am I doing? I can't have a conversation with you? You're so high and mighty you can't have a conversation with your own father? What's *wrong* with you?"

"Mom," Apple cried.

"Leave her alone!" her mother said from the kitchen.

He ignored her.

"I'm telling you. Marry someone smart. Someone like me. Like your mother did. Stupid people should always marry someone smart. That's my advice to you."

He picked up his car keys and left for work.

"Why did you marry him, Mom?"

"He was different then," her mother said.

"He wasn't like this?"

"He was nice to me then."

"For how long?"

"Until we were married."

"Did it start right away? Apple said.

"No, not right away. It started in bits. That's how you get pulled in. He'd be nice, and then he'd say something mean, and I would think that it was just him having a tough day on the job. Then he'd be nice again for days and I would forget about what he had said."

Apple nodded.

"But then the bad words started to come more often, and by then we had you and that's when things *really* got bad."

"Like they are now?"

"Yes," her mother said.

"Why didn't you leave him when it got bad? When I was a baby?"

"And go where? And do what? I depend on him for a place to live, food to eat, my clothes, everything."

"You could take a job," Apple said.

"I have no skills," her mother said.

"We could leave together, Mom."

"I can't. I just can't. I'm stuck. And he scares me."

"He doesn't scare me," Apple said. "He disgusts me."

"You should leave as soon as you can get out. Get out and take my advice. Don't *ever* get married. It's the worst thing in the world for a woman. You think you know someone until you marry them. It's all sweetness before the wedding, but then it turns rotten. Most men are monsters on the inside, but you can never tell which ones are and which ones aren't. I've seen it so many times. Have men friends, but promise me you'll never marry one of them. I don't want this life for you. It's no good."

Apple looked at the closed front door.

"I promise," she said.

"Never, ever. Okay?" her mother said.

"Never, ever," Apple said.

She got the tattoo on her eighteenth birthday.

The Mail

Carl the mailman had walked thousands of miles, and all of them in the same neighborhood. He was ready for retirement and looking forward to moving to Florida with his wife, Mary.

"When we get down there where the weather's good I'm going to get a golf cart and drive it everywhere," he told Mary. "I've walked enough for one lifetime."

"But it's kept you in good shape," Mary said. "I should walk more."

"Well, feel free to do my route anytime you'd like," Carl laughed.

"Oh, I think I'll leave the work to you," Mary said. "I like it on the couch."

They had been married for 45 years and had no children, which made the decision to head to Florida an easy one.

Carl sorted the Kepler's mail as he walked toward the mailbox next to their front door. One of the letters caught his eye because of the sloppy writing, all in pencil. It was unusual to see a letter addressed in pencil.

He dropped it into the box and reversed his steps down their walkway.

"This one's for you," Hannah's mother said, handing her the penciled envelope.

Hannah stared at it.

"Who is it from?" her mother said.

"I don't know," Hannah said.

"Well, open it."

"Maybe later."

"Who writes to you in pencil?" her mother said. "You're getting so many of those pencil letters. Who does that? It's not proper. They should use a pen. Tell them to use a pen. Who is this friend of yours that doesn't use a pen? What's wrong with this person?"

"Maybe they don't have a pen," Hannah said.

"Why do you always have to annoy me?" her mother said. "You with your smart answers. Maybe they don't have a *pen*. Who doesn't have a pen?"

Hannah went to her room.

And opened the letter.

It read:

Your ugly and I hope you dye. Nobody likes you.

There was a brown smear across the bottom of the letter.

Hannah smelled it. "Poop," she said.

She went into the bathroom and flushed the letter, as she had all the others.

Margaret

"Do you read books, Popeye?"

They were 82 houses into Route 1. Long John Nebel was reading a NoDoz commercial.

"No."

"Why not?"

"I guess because they made me read them in school and I hated taking tests about them."

"I think you'd like reading *In Watermelon Sugar*."

"Who wrote it?"

"Richard Brautigan."

"Who's he?" Brian said.

"He's the man who wrote *In Watermelon Sugar*," Hannah said.

"Oh."

"You should read it," Hannah said.

"Why?"

"Because it's sad and beautiful."

"How can it be both of those things?"

"Some books are just like that," Hannah said. "They make you think, and cry."

"Why would you want to read something that makes you cry? Why don't you read something that's *happy* and beautiful?" Brian said.

"There are those books, too, but Richard Brautigan's books are good to read because he makes you imagine a world that's different from this world."

"How can a world be different from this world?" Brian said.

"It can be different because of imagination."

"Oh."

"You have an imagination. I've seen it. You like to imagine the things Long John is telling you about."

"Ole Olson made me imagine a roomful of woman's breasts," Brian said.

"Yes," Hannah said.

"Tell me what the watermelon book is about."

"Wouldn't you rather read it yourself?"

"No," Brian said. "I like when you tell me about things."

"Okay, a man tells the story."

"What's his name?" Brian said.

"He doesn't have a name. He says that his name is whatever you want it to be."

"Really?"

"Yes," Hannah said. "You have to use your imagination."

"You can do that?" Brian said. "Have no name?"

"Sure," Hannah said.

"So what does the man do?"

"He's writing a book."

"What is the book about?" Brian said.

"He won't tell anyone. He's just writing it, but he doesn't know if he'll ever finish it. He lives in a place called iDEATH."

"I death?" Brian said.

"Yes, but it's spelled funny. It's all one word. The i is small and the rest is capital letters. And both words are connected."

"Why is it spelled like that?"

"I don't know. It's what's in Richard Brautigan's imagination."

"Okay."

"There are hardly any books in iDEATH, and just about everything is made of watermelon sugar."

"Really," Brian said. "Can you make things out of watermelon sugar?"

"You can in the story. That's imagination," Hannah said

"What does iDEATH mean?"

"He doesn't tell that, but a lot of people die there as the story goes on."

"How?"

"They kill themselves with pocket knives. The cut off their thumbs, and then their ears, and their noses. And they bleed to death."

"Why?"

"Because they're drunk on whiskey that they make from old junk."

"Can you do that?"

"What?"

"Make whiskey from old junk," Brian said.

"It's imagination." Hannah said.

"Why do they kill themselves?"

"Because the talking tigers used to kill them and eat them. That was their nature. They would apologize for doing it. But then the people killed all the tigers and built a fish hatchery over the bones of the very last tiger they killed. The people who killed themselves thought the other people were too nice, and that there wasn't enough death. So they made more of it."

"Death?" Brian said.

"Yes."

"That's crazy."

"The people who didn't kill themselves also liked to bury their dead in glass coffins that were under the water. The trout would watch as the people did the funerals. The people could visit the dead and see the trout at the same time."

"This is a very strange place," Brian said.

"It is, and the man with no name was making love with Margaret. She had a best friend called Pauline, but then the man with no name switched from Margaret to Pauline and Margaret was very sad."

"So what happened to Margaret?"

"She died."

"Did Pauline also die?" Brian said.

"I don't know. She's still alive when the book runs out of pages. Books never really end. You can imagine whatever you'd like after you get to the last page of any book. That's the nice thing about books. They become a part of you when you reach their end. They sit and wait for you to continue the story for them."

"You mean like the book gets tired of talking?" Brian said.

"Yes," Hannah said. "Like we get tired from doing the milk. Books are alive, just like we are. They run out of pages like people run out of days. When someone dies, other people keep talking about them, even though the person is not there anymore. People are like books in that way. The story goes on. Stories are made of energy. Everything is."

"How do you think of these things?"

"What things?" Hannah said.

"About books and all the other stuff you talk to me about. How do you think of it all?"

"I don't think about it, Popeye. It's just there."

"Where?"

"Everywhere. It's energy. It's always there. You just have to pay attention to it and do what it tells you to do."

"Really?"

"Yes, and you get to make up your own ending when you read books. You just have to keep reading the energy, but without the pages."

"I don't have to read the watermelon book now," Brian said.

"Why not?"

"Because you told me all about it."

"But I didn't tell you about my ending for it."

"Will you tell me?"

"I'll show you," Hannah said.

"When?"

"I don't know yet."

"Okay," Brian said.

"Maybe you'll read a book on your own someday," Hannah said.

"Maybe I will. Or maybe you'll read another book and tell me about it."

"Do you want to be my daytime friend, Popeye?" Hannah said.

"What do you mean?" Brian said.

"Can we be friends during the daytime? We're nighttime and early-morning friends now."

"I guess we could," Brian said. "What would we do in the daytime?"

"We could go for walks," Hannah said. "And maybe get married."

"Oh, I don't know, Hannah."

"Why?"

"We have to be careful. Richie told me that."

"Careful about what?" Hannah said.

"I don't know," Brian said, embarrassed. "We should just be careful with each other, I guess. I think it would be better if we weren't daytime friends."

Hannah stared out the windshield as Brian pulled up to the Spence house.

"They get four quarts of whole milk," he said, without looking at her.

"Okay," Hannah said as she slid out of the truck.

"Will you marry me, Popeye?"

"What?"

"Will you marry me?"

"I can't.

"Why not?"

"You're too young," Brian said.

"I'm allowed to get married at fourteen. It's the law. I read that in the library. I'm fifteen now."

"You're too young," Brian said.

"I'm not," Hannah said.

"*I'm* too young," Brian said

"You're old, Popeye."

"I'm eighteen."

"I know," Hanna said. "Marry me and we'll be friends forever. We'll teach each other things and we'll do the milk every night. Forever and ever."

"I can't marry you, Hannah. I have to take care of my mother."

"Popeye married Olive," Hannah said.

"I know, but I can't marry you."

"Why not?"

"I don't love you. You're my friend."

When he dropped her off at her house, her parents were still asleep, as they always were when he dropped her off.

Hannah undressed and showered. She washed her hair and combed it after she toweled off. She left her hair wet and put on a white granny dress, sandals, and a straw hat with a wide brim. It had a red, artificial rose on its side.

Her mother was having coffee at the kitchen table.

"Did you wash your face?" she said.

Hannah didn't answer.

"I said, did you wash your face?"

"I showered," Hannah said.

"But did you wash your face?"

"Yes."

"What soap did you use?"

"I used what was there."

"Did you scrub? Your pimples aren't going to go away unless you scrub."

"I scrubbed."

"Why didn't you dry your hair. It looks stringy."

"I like the way it feels," Hannah said.

"You should dry your hair."

"I spend the nights delivering milk on a truck," Hannah said.

"Don't be ridiculous," her mother said. "Why do you say such stupid things to me?"

"And also juice, and eggs, and other things. I deliver it all to two-hundred houses. I do it every night. While you're sleeping."

"Stop annoying me with your made-up stories. They're not funny."

Hannah walked toward the door.

"Where are you going?" her mother said.

"I don't know yet," Hannah said.

"When will you be back?"

"I don't know yet."

"Well, behave yourself," her mother said.

Hannah left.

She walked nearly to the end of the railroad platform, sat on the concrete with her long legs stretched out, and waited for the trains to go by. Some stopped; others blasted right through with horns blaring. The platform shook when these went by.

"So much energy," Hannah whispered. "So much . . ."

She wondered when the next one would arrive.

A pigeon landed near her.

Hannah smiled at it.

It stepped closer to her.

Her lips moved, as if in prayer.

The pigeon stepped closer.

Hannah opened her hand and laid it on the concrete, palm up.

The pigeon stepped onto her hand and nested.

"What is it like to fly?" Hannah whispered and went very still.

"That must be nice," she said after a long moment.

"Do you feel free?"

"Yes."

"That's nice. Thank you for sharing with me, beautiful bird."

A train was coming.

Would it stop?

Or would it go by fast?

And with so much energy.

So much.

She waited.

The Note

Brian walked to the backyard and opened the cooler. The route book wasn't there, but there was a note:

I have sold the route and your services are no longer needed. Leave the route book in the picnic cooler. Drive the truck to the plant and leave it there with the keys under the floor mat. The new owner will pick up the truck later today. He will not offer you a job because I told him that you caused me to lose too many of my customers through your bad behavior.
DO NOT KNOCK ON MY DOOR!!!

Brian opened some of the envelopes and counted out his pay.

Later On

He wondered if Hannah was worried about him. He hadn't picked her up to do the milk for a while, of course. He'd never again pick her up to do that, but she didn't know he had lost his job, and he had no way of getting in touch with her, unless he went to her house and knocked on the door.

But Richie had told him to be careful. He hadn't done anything wrong, but what might her parents think if he showed up and said he wanted to see her. He was so much older than she was. Three whole years. What would they think? Would he be in more trouble than he already was? He had been going to the businesses on Division Avenue for the past few days, asking if they had any work for him in the warehouse. No luck so far, and his mother was getting worried.

It couldn't hurt to just drive by Hannah's house, could it? Maybe she would be outside and he could talk to her for a moment. Just for a moment. To explain what had happened. To tell her that he wouldn't be able to be with her anymore. He wasn't a milkman anymore and she was too young to be with him. He couldn't marry her. He didn't love her. He was her friend, but he wasn't sure if he could be her friend anymore. He was confused.

He sat across the street from the Kepler's house in his Rambler American and watched the people come and go. As each person approached the front door, they stopped by a pitcher of water that was next to a basin on a small table. Each person poured a bit of the water on their hands and used the paper towels that were next to the basin to dry their hands. They put the used paper towels in the small garbage pail that was on the stoop next to the small table. Then they went into the house without knocking.

Brian had never seen people do this. Why were they doing this?

He sat for an hour and watched more people come and go. Some people brought what looked like bakery boxes. He could tell by the string used to tie the boxes closed. He wondered what was in those boxes. Cake? Pie?

Why?

Some people were crying when they arrived.

Why?

He waited another hour, but Hannah never appeared.

He never saw her again.

The next day, he went to Pathmark to see if they were hiring. They were!

Delaney's
2018

"I have to be going, but would you like to have dinner with me sometime?" Brian said. "No strings. I just enjoy your company."

She smiled. "Aren't you afraid of my father?"

"No."

"Good," Apple said. "Neither am I. Not anymore. If he comes back in here tomorrow, I'm calling the cops."

"Good. And we won't include him in our dinner date," Brian said.

Apple laughed.

"Saturday night work for you?" Brian said.

"What are you intentions, sir?" Apple smiled.

"I'm thinking Italian," Brian said. "But you choose."

She laughed again.

"And I absolutely promise *not* to propose marriage during dessert," Brian said.

"Oh, what the hell," Apple said. She reached for a pen and a Delaney's business card and wrote her phone number on the back of it. She handed it to him.

"Call me on Friday," she said. "Italian sounds nice."

He held out his hand for the pen and wrote Apple above her phone number.

"What's your last name?" he said, smiling.

"Thanatos."

"Spell it for me."

"T-H-A-N-A-T-O-S."

Brian wrote it on the card.

"That's Greek, right?" he said looking up.

"Yes."

"Also your father's name?"

"Unfortunately, yes."

"It goes well with Apple."

"And even better with Apollonia," she said.

"It does. Does it mean something in Greek?"

"It means death." She leaned in on her elbows, and smirked.

"Really?"

"Yes, just another gift from Daddy. But don't let that get in your way," she winked.

"It never has. Well, so far it hasn't," Brian chuckled.

"Yeah, it's not like he's gonna kill you for taking me out to dinner."

"Let's hope not," Brian said.

"Books never really end. You can imagine whatever you'd like after you get to the last page of any book. That's the nice thing about books. They become a part of you when you reach their end. They sit and wait for you to continue the story for them."

- Hannah Kepler

Made in the USA
Columbia, SC
29 April 2025